The Princess Plays

by Colleen Neuman

Baker's Plays
7611 Sunset Blvd.
Los Angeles, CA 90042
bakersplays.com

*These plays are for the children who performed them,
especially Megan, Max and Kristen.*

THE PRINCESS AND THE PRINCESS
Flexible cast of 21
One simple set
30 minute playing time

The Princess and the Princess was first performed by the students at Wrightstown High School, Wrightstown, WI on May 5, 1991 with the following cast:

```
THE LADY WHO TELLS THE STORY . . . . . . Ann Busse
TWINKLEBERRY . . . . . . . . . . . . . . . . . Rosanne Koltz
POPPLEPEA . . . . . . . . . . . . . . . . . . . . Sarah Thomas
ROYAL GUARD 1 . . . . . . . . . . . . . . . . . Patty Clancy
ROYAL GUARD 2 . . . . . . . . . . . . . . . . . Sara Busse
ROYAL GUARD 3 . . . . . . . . . . . . . . . . Dawn Gibson
GENERAL GOOGE . . . . . . . . . . . . . . . . Tony Kille
SOLDIER 1  . . . . . . . . . . . . . . . . . . . . Max Neuman
SOLDIER 2  . . . . . . . . . . . . . . . . Jenny Vander Heiden
SOLDIER 3  . . . . . . . . . . . . . . . . . Steve Leurquin
SOLDIER 4  . . . . . . . . . . . . . . . . . . Jeanine Zelten
SOLDIER 5  . . . . . . . . . . . . . . . . . . . Eric Gerend
QUEEN . . . . . . . . . . . . . . . . . . . . . Lisa Liebergen
LADY-IN-WAITING 1  . . . . . . . . . . Laurie Rotzenberg
LADY-IN-WAITING 2  . . . . . . . . . . Jenny Steinberger
LADY-IN-WAITING 3  . . . . . . . . . . . . Shelly Pagel
LADY-IN-WAITING 4  . . . . . . . . . . . . Melissa Moss
LADY-IN-WAITING 5  . . . . . . . . . . Terry Jo Albers
LADY-IN-WAITING 6  . . . . . . . . . . . . . Liz Baker
STAGEHAND . . . . . . . . . . . . . . . . . . Leanne Pahl
ROYAL WISE PERSON  . . . . . . . . . . . Megan Neuman
```

CHARACTERS

THE LADY WHO TELLS THE STORY
TWINKLEBERRY
POPPLEPEA
ROYAL GUARD 1
ROYAL GUARD 2
ROYAL GUARD 3
GENERAL GOOGE
SOLDIER 1
SOLDIER 2
SOLDIER 3
SOLDIER 4
SOLDIER 5
QUEEN
LADY-IN-WAITING 1
LADY-IN-WAITING 2
LADY-IN-WAITING 3
LADY-IN-WAITING 4
LADY-IN-WAITING 5
LADY-IN-WAITING 6
STAGEHAND
ROYAL WISE PERSON

Note: The number of Royal Guards, Soldiers and Ladies-in-Waiting is flexible. Just redistribute the lines to accommodate more or fewer performers.

THE PRINCESS AND THE PRINCESS

(A large, overstuffed armchair covered in big flowered fabric is centered on the floor in front of the stage.

On stage, there is a simple backdrop depicting a mountain scene placed directly behind the curtain. Stage Left, there is a small pretty shelf for TWINKLEBERRY's mirror. The shelf may also have a few perfume bottles, a jewelry box, etc. on it. Stage Right, there is a coat rack. The sash to POPPLEPEA's dress is hanging on one of the hooks, her basket is on another. The egg is on the stage floor a step or two from the coat rack.

If necessary, the entire play can be performed in front of a closed curtain, providing there is about two feet of space between the curtain and the edge of the stage.

You may want to have a special "Children Only" seating area on the floor in front of THE LADY WHO TELLS THE STORY's chair.

Sweet, child-like MUSIC begins. THE LADY WHO TELLS THE STORY enters from Stage Left, pushing her lawnmower. She mows the floor in front of the stage, going carefully around her chair, making very square corners — all with real concentration. She seems oblivious to the audience. After finishing a row or two, she notices a child seated near the front. She slows down, music goes down. She leans over and "reads" from the child's forehead.)

THE LADY WHO TELLS THE STORY. (*Reads slowly, turning the child's face this way and that to get all the words.*) (*Your theater group*) presents "The Princess And The Princess." (*Straightens up.*) That's a very odd thing to have written on your forehead. If I were you, I'd go home and wash my face. (*Resumes mowing, music comes back up. Notices another child, preferably at the other side of the audience. Stops mowing, music goes down. Leans over and "reads" again.*) I am a very good boy/girl and should be given two desserts. (*Straightens up. Looks disapproving.*) I think that's a very bad idea. You're too small to have two desserts. (*Starts to turn away, turns back.*) If anyone ever gives you two desserts, you should give one of them to me. (*Mows over to chair, music is back up. Music fades away as she parks lawnmower.*) Well, I'm very tired and I don't know if I feel like a story. (*Collapses in chair.*) I worked very hard today. I weeded the marshmallows and mowed the cabbages. (*Has removed one shoe and is rubbing foot.*) My feet hurt, my head hurts (*Pointedly to one child.*) and, NO, I will not be taking off my hat. (*Suspiciously.*) I know your type. You'd like this hat, wouldn't you? (*Pulling it down and tying it tighter.*) Well, you're not going to get it. (*Settles herself.*) Did I tell you I mowed the cabbages? Very hard work. (*Opens purse, drags out hanky, mops face.*) They always fight back and holler about it. And then, as if that wasn't enough, that dreadful rabbit family from next door would stop by and go on and on about their trip to Florida. I had to look at all their pictures. (*Leaning forward.*) Have you ever seen any pictures of Florida? They're all the same — blue on the top which is the sky and blue on the bottom which is the water. (*Falls back, eyes glaze over. With great feeling.*) The rabbits had hundreds of them. Do any of you live next door to rabbits? (*To a child who says, "No."*) Well, you're lucky. (*To a child who says, "Yes."*) And I feel sorry for you.

(*An enormous yawn.*)   Yes, I'm much too tired for a story. You'll have to go away and come back another time. (*Curls up, tips hat over face, goes to sleep. After a moment she pushes hat back and peeks out.*) Oh, don't look at me like that. We'll have a story tomorrow. I promise. Two if you're good. That means even if you're bad, you get one. (*Very pleased with herself. Curls up again, pulls hat down. After a moment, peeks out again.*)   You're still here!   Why haven't you gone home? (*Relents.*) Oh, all right, all right. If you're going to make a face about it — one story. But only if you promise to eat all your chocolate for breakfast tomorrow. You do eat chocolate for breakfast, don't you? Because if you don't (*Growing alarm.*) you might be rabbits in disguise! (*Jumps up, very alarmed.*) You don't eat lettuce, do you? (*Lets children respond.*) Well, you better not. Now, all together — I promise to eat chocolate for breakfast. (*Children say it with her.*)   Well (*Somewhat reluctantly.*) all right. Here's your story. (*Sits. Picks up book.*) But you better pay attention because it's going to go by very fast! (*Opens book.*) Once upon a time ... (*Stops reading. Lowers book.*) You know it doesn't work unless we all say it together. I'll give you one more chance and then I'm going to go read it to the cabbages. Maybe then they'll start speaking to me again. All together now — Once upon a time (*Children all say it with her. When THE LADY speaks her next line it is with a sense of wonder and enchantment — the way all stories should be told.*) there was a princess ...

(*TWINKLEBERRY enters from Stage Left, carrying her hand mirror. She walks on a few steps, holds up mirror and looks at herself in it — very vain and arrogant. Freeze.*)

... and a princess.

> (*POPPLEPEA enters from Stage Right, holding her old evening gown on a hanger. She walks on a few steps, holds up the gown to admire it — a sweet smile. Freeze.*)

The first princess ...

> (*TWINKLEBERRY unfreezes. Uses the mirror to primp, perhaps put on a squirt of perfume, add a bracelet from her shelf. Very taken with herself.*)

... was very rich. She wore a fancy dress everyday, not just on Sunday. Her hair was curled, her nose was powdered, her wrists were perfumed and she wore gold and diamonds just because she felt like it. Everyday the rich princess, whose name was Twinkleberry, would go to the shops to buy things like -
TWINKLEBERRY. Ostrich feathers! I simply must have some ostrich feathers to wear in my hair. (*Sets mirror on shelf and freezes.*)
The Lady. (*Doesn't think much of TWINKLEBERRY.*) Hmmmppph! (*Resumes her storytelling tone.*) The other princess ...

> (*POPPLEPEA unfreezes. She hangs dress on coat rack, straightens it lovingly. Takes sash off hook and ties it at her waist. Picks up basket, finds egg and puts it in basket.*)

... was not rich at all. She had just one fancy dress left and it was worn paper thin so she only wore it on Sundays and then just for lunch. The rest of the week she wore a dress she made herself from flour sacks. She didn't have powder or perfume or gold or diamonds but she did have a chicken so everyday the princess, whose name was Popplepea, went to market to sell eggs. One day ...

> (*POPPLEPEA begins a slow stroll to Center Stage, looking up at the sky. Curtain opens slowly behind her.*)

Popplepea left a little early for the market and Twinkleberry left a little late (*TWINKLEBERRY looks at watch, gasps, hurries toward Center Stage.*) for the shops and they bumped ...

> (*POPPLEPEA and TWINKLEBERRY bump into each other at Center Stage.*)

... into each other.

> (*As the action Onstage begins, THE LADY should continue reading, eating, changing positions in her chair and so on. She shouldn't distract from what's happening Onstage but she shouldn't be static either.*)

TWINKLEBERRY. (*Irate.*) How dare you!
POPPLEPEA. (*Pleasant, polite, with an understated regal air.*) I beg your pardon?
TWINKLEBERRY. You clumsy oaf! You've mussed my dress! I see a wrinkle! And here's another one! Oh! And another one!
POPPLEPEA. Don't be silly. I've hardly touched you. And your dress is fine.

TWINKLEBERRY. It is not fine! It's wrinkled! You've ruined it! I should go home and change but I don't have time! You've made me late! Now move aside and let me pass! (*TWINKLEBERRY leans at POPPLEPEA, POPPLEPEA leans back and they freeze.*)

THE LADY. (*Eating a sandwich, gets up, strolls to stage.*) You see, the path curved around a mountain ledge here and was very narrow. Well, you can see how narrow it is. To one side there was a sheer cliff that went straight up (*Looking straight up.*) and to the other side was a sheer cliff that went straight down (*Looking straight down.*) so only one person could pass at a time. And, of course (*Strolls back to chair.*) it was the law of the land that everyone must allow a princess (*Sits.*) to pass first.

POPPLEPEA. (*Still pleasant.*) Let you pass? On the contrary, I think the proper etiquette would be for you to let me pass. I, after all, am a princess.

TWINKLEBERRY. You?! A princess?! (*Laughs very hard, wiping away tears, slapping leg and so on. Then stops dead.*) Don't make me laugh. You're a raggedy little peasant girl in flour sacking and barefeet. Now go back the way you've come so that I may pass.

POPPLEPEA. (*With dignity.*) I may be barefoot and I may be dressed in flour sacks but I am a princess — Princess Popplepea of the Kingdom of Shroppelham.

TWINKLEBERRY. Shroppelham? Huh! Never heard of it.

POPPLEPEA. Well, we were very big in the twelfth century. It's been pretty much all downhill since then.

TWINKLEBERRY. I thought so! You're poor as a church mouse and if you're poor you can't be a princess. And if you insist on pretending to be a princess I'll have you arrested.

POPPLEPEA. (*Not worried.*) On what charge?

TWINKLEBERRY. Impersonating a princess while blocking

a public thoroughfare and that's a felony.

POPPLEPEA. That's nonsense.

TWINKLEBERRY. Oh, nonsense, is it? We'll just see about that. (*Yelling her head off.*) Help! Help! Princess in distress! Princess in distress! Help, help, help, help, help! Princess in distress! Princess in distress! (*ROYAL GUARD 1, 2 and 3 enter from Stage Left. Running and out of breath.*)

ROYAL GUARD 1. Yes, Your Highness?

ROYAL GUARD 2. Are you in distress, Your Highness?

ROYAL GUARD 3. We heard you shrieking way back at the castle. (*ROYAL GUARD 1, 2 and 3 line up in that order to TWINKLEBERRY's left.*)

TWINKLEBERRY. (*Shrieking.*) I never shriek! (*Regains composure. Becomes very regal.*) And, of course, I'm in distress. Arrest this (*Extreme distaste.*) person. (*Each ROYAL GUARD leans forward to look around TWINKLEBERRY on these lines.*)

ROYAL GUARD 1. What?

ROYAL GUARD 2. Who?

ROYAL GUARD 3. Her?

TWINKLEBERRY. Yes, her. Arrest her. Immediately!

ROYAL GUARD 1. On what charge?

TWINKLEBERRY. Impersonating a princess while blocking a public thoroughfare.

ROYAL GUARD 1. Ooooh, that's very serious.

ROYAL GUARD 2. It certainly is — it's a felony!

ROYAL GUARD 3. (*To POPPLEPEA.*) You should be ashamed of yourself.

POPPLEPEA. I am not blocking a public thoroughfare any more than she is, and I am a princess.

ROYAL GUARD 3. Are you?

ROYAL GUARD 2. Really?

ROYAL GUARD 1. She is?

POPPLEPEA. And if you arrest me you'll be guilty of a felony.

ROYAL GUARD 1. We will?

ROYAL GUARD 3. Are you sure?

ROYAL GUARD 2. Which one?

POPPLEPEA. False imprisonment of a princess.

ROYAL GUARD 1. Ooooh, that's a bad one.

ROYAL GUARD 2. We could go to prison.

ROYAL GUARD 3. (*To TWINKLEBERRY.*) You didn't tell us she was a princess.

TWINKLEBERRY. (*Enraged.*) AR-REST HER!

ROYAL GUARD 1. Oh, all right then. (*Peeks over at POPPLEPEA, clears throat, speaks with absolutely no conviction.*) You're arrested.

POPPLEPEA. No, I'm not.

TWINKLEBERRY. You call that arresting somebody?

ROYAL GUARD 2. She's not done yet.

ROYAL GUARD 3. Let her finish.

ROYAL GUARD 1. (*Holding out handcuffs toward POPPLEPEA.*) Here. Put these on.

POPPLEPEA. (*Looks at them a moment, considers it, decides.*) No.

ROYAL GUARD 1. (*Astonished.*) No?

POPPLEPEA. (*Definite.*) No.

ROYAL GUARD 1. (*To ROYAL GUARD 2.*) She said no!

ROYAL GUARD 2. No one's ever said no before, (*To ROYAL GUARD 3.*) have they?

ROYAL GUARD 3. No. No one ever has. (*To POPPLEPEA.*) Are you sure you can do that?

POPPLEPEA. Quite sure. I'm a princess.

ROYAL GUARD 3. She says she's quite sure.

ROYAL GUARD 1. Well, of course she's sure.

ROYAL GUARD 2. She's a princess, isn't she?

TWINKLEBERRY. (*Blows up.*) AAAAAAAAAA! Enough!
Go back to the castle! I'll handle this myself! (*In a huff, she
turns her back to them, folds arms. Very reluctantly, fearfully,
ROYAL GUARD 1 taps TWINKLEBERRY on the shoulder.
TWINKLEBERRY does a slow, cold turn and stares at them.*)
You're still here.

ROYAL GUARD 1. (*Nervous.*) Excuse me, Your Highness,
but are you by any chance still in distress?

TWINKLEBERRY. YES!!!

ROYAL GUARD 2. (*Nervous, cowering back.*) Then we can't
leave. We're members of the Royal Guard.

ROYAL GUARD 3. (*Also nervous, cowering.*) And we must
never leave a princess in distress. We took an oath.

TWINKLEBERRY.   (*Exploding.*)   AAAAAAAAAAA!
Where's my cavalry, my infantry? I want my army, my navy!
I want my royal balloonists!

(*GENERAL GOOGE and SOLDIERS 1, 2, 3, 4 and 5
come charging on from Stage Left. Have them zigzag
across the stage behind the scenery a few times, really
pounding their feet, so the audience hears them coming.
The GENERAL comes on first and stands to ROYAL
GUARD 3's left. The SOLDIERS line up in numerical
order to the GENERAL's left.*)

GENERAL. (*A little out of breath, very abject.*) General
Googe reporting, Your Royal Majesty Highness Ma'am. A
thousand apologies for taking so long. We were on maneuvers.
(*Catches his breath a little. Then, hopefully.*) Would you like us
to do battle for you?

TWINKLEBERRY. Yes!

GENERAL. (*Even more hopefully.*) Do we get to use our weapons?

TWINKLEBERRY. Yes!!

GENERAL. (*To SOLDIERS.*) We get to use our weapons! (*Great hollering and cheering from SOLDIERS. To TWINKLEBERRY.*) We are deeply grateful, Your Majesty. Now, where's the enemy?

TWINKLEBERRY. (*Pointing.*) There!

GENERAL. (*Looking around.*) Where?

TWINKLEBERRY. There!

GENERAL. Well, yes, I do see the one but where are all the rest?

TWINKLEBERRY. There aren't anymore! She's it! Attack!

GENERAL. Yes, Your Majestyness. (*To SOLDIERS.*) Men! Brandish arms! (*All draw swords.*) AAAAAAAATTACK! (*Much shouting and waving of swords and stomping of feet but no one moves. Stop.*) Uh, excuse us, Majesty. We can't quite get at her this way. If you could just move ...

TWINKLEBERRY. Move? Me move? That's how this started! I won't move! I'll never move! Make her move!

GENERAL. (*Shaken, bowing in apology.*) Oh yes, yes. Whatever you say, Your Royal Highnessnessness. (*To SOLDIERS.*) Men, CHAAAARRRGE! (*Even more shouting and waving and stomping but nobody moves. Stop. SOLDIERS whisper together.*)

TWINKLEBERRY. (*A little weary.*) Well, go on. Charge then.

GENERAL. We can't quite seem to make any headway, Majesty.

SOLDIER 1. Well, actually, we could, sir.

GENERAL. Could what?

SOLDIER 2. Make headway, sir.

GENERAL. What's that? We could? How?

SOLDIER 3. We could charge back!

GENERAL. Back?

SOLDIER 4. Yes sir. It's Soldier Number 5's idea.

GENERAL. Soldier Number 5? Which one is he?

SOLDIER 5. (*Raising hand.*) Here sir! (*Other SOLDIERS are pointing to him.*)

GENERAL. I see. Now what's all this about charging back?

SOLDIER 5. Well, you see, sir, there's no one in our way back there. (*Looking back the way they've come.*) We'd have a clear path. We could charge and charge and charge and never run into anybody. (*All SOLDIERS are looking at the GENERAL very hopefully.*)

GENERAL. (*Sarcastically.*) So, you all want to charge back, eh? (*SOLDIERS nod eagerly.*) Charging back would be ... retreat! And I'll never retreat! I'd be disgraced! My reputation as a general, as a hero would be ruined! (*Even worse.*) They'd take away my shiny stuff. (*Puts a protective hand over his shiny shoulder trim. SOLDIERS are repentant.*)

SOLDIER 1. Oh, we hadn't thought of that.

SOLDIER 2. Well, that's no good then.

SOLDIER 4. Never mind.

SOLDIER 3. We'll never mention it again. Bad Soldier Number 5. (*SOLDIERS 1, 2, 3 and 4 glare at SOLDIER 5.*)

TWINKLEBERRY. Are you going to charge — or not?

GENERAL. (*Very penitent.*) We'd like to charge, we'd love to charge but — oh, a thousand thousand apologies, Your Royal Majesticness — we can't.

TWINKLEBERRY. (*Exploding.*) How dare you disobey me!? I'll have you court-martialled! I'll have you hung from the highest yardarm! I don't even know what a yardarm is but I'll find out and I'll get one and I'll hang you from it … ! (*QUEEN enters from Stage Left followed by her LADIES-IN-WAITING in numerical order. QUEEN stands to left of SOLDIER 5.*)

QUEEN. (*As she enters.*) Yoo-hoo, dear! (*ROYAL GUARD, GENERAL and SOLDIERS kneel and bow heads.*)

TWINKLEBERRY. (*Not happy to see the QUEEN.*) Mother! What are you doing up here?

QUEEN. (*Casually, to ROYAL GUARD, GENERAL and SOLDIERS.*) Oh, up, up. (*ROYAL GUARD, GENERAL and SOLDIERS stand as before. To TWINKLEBERRY.*) The ladies and I were bored. There's no one down at the castle and now I see why — you're all up here playing some sort of game. It looks like great fun. May we play?

TWINKLEBERRY. (*Clenched teeth.*) It's not a game, Mother.

QUEEN. (*Disappointed.*) Oh. Too bad.

LADY 1. Not a game?

LADY 3. It looks like a game.

LADY 5. It looks like "Leap Dragon!" (*LADIES speak with increasing excitement.*)

LADY 4. Or "Follow The Fool!"

LADY 2. Or "Upsy Dupsy!"

LADY 6. Oooh, I love "Upsy Dupsy!"

TWINKLEBERRY. It's not a game!

QUEEN. Fine, dear. (*To LADIES, gently.*) Ladies, it's not a game. (*LADIES begin to sniffle.*)

LADY 3. Oh, it's not a game.

LADY 1. I'm so disappointed.

LADY 5. I don't think I can bear it. (*LADIES are all crying.*)

QUEEN. (*Pats LADY 1.*) There, there Ladies. (*To TWINKLEBERRY.*) Really, dear, I wish you wouldn't promise a game if there isn't going to be a game. You know how upset they get.

TWINKLEBERRY. I never promised anybody a game!

QUEEN. Well, never mind that. Did you enjoy shopping?

TWINKLEBERRY. No, Mother, I didn't enjoy shopping.

QUEEN. There's no need to get testy about it, dear. I never enjoy shopping. I think it's a bore.

TWINKLEBERRY. Mother, I haven't been shopping yet because this mousy little peasant girl is in the path and won't move!

QUEEN. (*Noticing POPPLEPEA for the first time.*) Oh hello.

POPPLEPEA. (*Very courteous, deep curtsey.*) Good morning, Your Majesty.

QUEEN. Well, she seems very pleasant. Did you ask nicely?

TWINKLEBERRY. Mother!

QUEEN. Did you say please?

TWINKLEBERRY. No!

QUEEN. Well, did you at least say excuse me?

TWINKLEBERRY. Mother, she's a peasant!

POPPLEPEA. Excuse me, Your Majesty, I'm not a peasant. I'm a princess.

QUEEN. Oh, are you?

POPPLEPEA. Yes, I am. I'm your daughter's equal and I won't move. Unless, of course, she does.

QUEEN. Well, there's the solution then. You'll both move.

TWINKLEBERRY. I will not!

POPPLEPEA. And if she doesn't, with all due respect, Your Majesty, I won't.

QUEEN. Yes, I see your point.

TWINKLEBERRY. Mother!

QUEEN. I see your point, too, dear. Well, at any rate,

Ladies, back to the castle. No one up here is having any fun and it's getting cold. (*LADIES don't move.*) Go ahead, Ladies.

LADY 1. Oh, but we can't, Your Highness.

QUEEN. Of course you can. Just follow back along the path the way we came.

LADY 2. But we're Ladies-in-Waiting.

QUEEN. I know that.

LADY 3. We have to wait. For you.

QUEEN. For me?

LADY 4. You always go first while we wait ...

LADY 5. ... and then we follow ...

LADY 6. ... you.

QUEEN. Ladies, if I go first I shall almost certainly plunge to my death. (*LADIES begin to sniffle.*)

LADY 2. Oh, we know.

LADY 4. It's so horrible.

LADY 6. A great tragedy.

LADIES 1, 2, 3, 4, 5, 6. (*In unison.*) And we'll all have to follow you! (*They collapse in tears, throw arms around each other, sob.*)

QUEEN. Oh dear. Let me think ...

LADY 3. (*Stops sobbing for a moment.*) We'll wait right here. (*Resumes sobbing.*)

QUEEN. I'm sure you will. Let's see — (*Looking at PRINCESSES.*) They won't move. (*Looking at the LADIES.*) They can't move. (*Looks up, looks down, realizes she's stuck.*) Oh bother.

THE LADY. (*She is now asleep in her chair in some very odd position.*) SNOOOOORRRREEEEEE! (*Snoring continues until she wakes up.*)

QUEEN. Oh! Lions!

ROYAL GUARD 2. No. It isn't lions. It's her.

SOLDIER 1. She's asleep again. (*CAST ad libs general mutterings of disgust. NOTE: "Cast" indicates performers Onstage and does not include THE LADY.*)

TWINKLEBERRY. She always falls asleep during this part. You'd think we were boring.

POPPLEPEA. No. She just likes to sleep. She must have mowed the cabbages today. They always wear her out.

QUEEN. Well, we have to finish. (*With a regal little hand gesture in the air.*) Wake her up I command it. (*CAST ad libs trying to wake up THE LADY. She sleeps on, snoring louder than ever. QUEEN snaps her fingers and CAST is immediately silent.*)

QUEEN. Oh, never mind. It's not working.

GENERAL. Last time she fell asleep we were stuck up here for three weeks.

LADY 5. (*With great feeling.*) And it snowed! (*LADIES all collapse in tears again, throw arms around each other, sob.*)

QUEEN. Well, the audience is going to have to help. (*With the regal hand gesture.*) I am the Queen. I command it. On the count of three you will all yell "Wake up!" Now all we need is someone who can count to three.

SOLDIER 1. (*Raising hand, jumping up and down, eager to be recognized.*) Oooh, ooh! Me, me! I know how, I know how!

QUEEN. Splendid, splendid — go ahead then.

SOLDIER 1. (*Struggling.*) Ah, ah, ah — how does it start?

SOLDIER 3. It starts with one.

SOLDIER 1. I knew that!

QUEEN. Never mind. (*To SOLDIER 3.*) You — you go ahead.

SOLDIER 3. (*Struggling.*) It starts with one. And then — ah, ah, ah ... (*With great effort.*) ... two! And then ... . oh, I always forget that last part.

SOLDIER 2. Me too.

QUEEN. We'll be here til Christmas! (*To audience.*) You'll have to do the counting too. All together now — we're going to count to three and then yell "Wake up!" (*Holding up her fingers for guidance. CAST counts and yells along with her.*) One - Two - Three - WAKE UP!!!! (*If the audience hasn't been very loud, THE LADY will sleep on, snoring louder than ever, twisting around into an even odder position.*)

QUEEN. Well, you weren't loud enough. We'll have to do it again. Remember to be really loud this time. All together (*CAST counts and yells with her.*) ONE - TWO - THREE - WAAAAAAAAKKE UUUUUUUPPP!!!!!

THE LADY. (*Wakes up with a leap into the air.*) What?!!! What's all the bloody shouting about? Don't you know shouting is rude? You'll upset the grownups. You know how they feel about shouting — (*jumps up on chair, stands on it, shouts at top of her lungs.*) THEY DON'T LIKE IT!!!! (*Becomes more ladylike.*) Now, if you would please control yourselves ... (*Sits on back of chair.*) I'm trying to read a story. (*Slides down to sitting position.*) You're lucky you didn't wake somebody up! (*Clears throat, resumes reading.*) And the Queen said, "Really, Twinkleberry, I wish you wouldn't ... (*QUEEN starts this line quietly, taking it over on the word "wish." THE LADY lets go of the line on the word "wish."*)

QUEEN. Really, Twinkleberry, I wish you wouldn't be so pigheaded.

TWINKLEBERRY. Pigheaded! How dare you!

QUEEN. I can dare anything I like. I'm the Queen, you're just a princess — I still outrank you.

TWINKLEBERRY. Well, I'm not pigheaded.

QUEEN. And I say you are.

TWINKLEBERRY. And I say I'm not! (*Stamping feet.*) I'm not, I'm not, I'm not, I'm not, I'm not!

QUEEN. You're being pigheaded right now. (*To SOLDIER 5.*) Isn't she being pigheaded?

SOLDIER 5. Well, she's being a little pigheaded.

ROYAL GUARD 2. She's being a lot pigheaded.

LADY 5. I've seen her much more pigheaded than this.

LADY 6. When?

LADY 5. All the time. (*CAST ad libs discussion of degrees of TWINKLEBERRY's pigheadedness.*)

QUEEN. (*After a few moments of the discussion, she snaps fingers. CAST is immediately silent. Speaks to audience.*) All of you out there — is she being pigheaded or not? All in favor of pigheaded, raise your hands. (*Some of the CAST raise their hands, others do not. Encourage the audience to follow their example. TWINKLEBERRY is glaring at audience.*) See there? You're pigheaded.

TWINKLEBERRY. Mother, they're peasants.

THE LADY. (*Out of patience with the whole situation. Jumps up.*) At least they're not rabbits! Get on with it! (*Reading.*) And the Queen said, "Here we are stuck on this horrid mountain ledge ..." (*THE LADY lets go of line and QUEEN takes it over on the word "horrid."*)

QUEEN. Here we are stuck on this horrid mountain ledge and the wind is picking up, (*SOUND EFFECT: Wind wildly howling. CAST all leans to one side as though blown by wind.*) the temperature is dropping (*CAST all start to shiver.*) ... and (*SOUND EFFECT: A crash of thunder.*) ... oh no! Now it's going to rain! (*SOUND EFFECT: Thunder continues.*)

POPPLEPEA. Excuse me, Your Highness, but why do you say that?

QUEEN. The thunder!

POPPLEPEA. (*Listens a moment.*) Oh, it's not going to rain.

QUEEN. How do you know?

POPPLEPEA. Because that's not thunder.

QUEEN. Oh, thank goodness.

POPPLEPEA. It's a rock slide.

CAST. A rock slide?! AAAAAAAAAAAAAAAA!!!! (*Freeze in an interesting collection of poses — some ducking, some clutching each other, some with mouths open, some bug-eyed etc. Thunder stops.*)

THE LADY. (*Stands, complains in a whiny sort of voice.*) Well, I just hate this part. (*Strolls along in front of audience.*) Those rocks come crashing down, squashing people in the audience, making a mess. Of course, if we had an audience of rabbits it wouldn't matter. I hate those rocks bouncing all over the place. Last time? One came this close to my hat. (*Thinks a moment. Decides. Shouts toward Stage Right.*) Hold the rocks!

STAGEHAND. (*Appears from behind curtain Stage Right. Eating a sandwich.*) Hold the rocks? What for?

THE LADY. I'm skipping ahead.

STAGEHAND. Oh no. Not again.

THE LADY. (*Flipping pages in book thoughtfully.*) We won't be needing the elephants ...

STAGEHAND. (*Shouting towards backstage.*) Eighty-six the elephants! (*SOUND EFFECT: Elephants roaring and trumpeting.*)

THE LADY. The camel races are out ...

STAGEHAND. Unsaddle the camels! (*SOUND EFFECT: Galloping going faster and faster.*) Catch that one! Catch it, catch it ...! (*SOUND EFFECT: An enormous crash that goes on and on and on. STAGEHAND and THE LADY react visually to crash. It finally stops. STAGEHAND peeks behind curtain.*) Oh man. Well, I'm not touching it. I cleaned up the last one.

(*To THE LADY.*) What about the snakes?

THE LADY. (*With an increasingly ominous tone.*) Oh, you mean the pythons and boa constrictors and eighteen-foot green cobras we hung from the ceiling to fall down on the audience at the bottom of page thirty-two? (*SOUND EFFECT: Hissing. THE LADY and STAGEHAND are both looking up over the heads of the audience.*)

STAGEHAND. Mmmm-hmmmmmmm.

THE LADY. (*A significant pause.*) Nah.

STAGEHAND. Roll up the snakes!

THE LADY. (*Has found a certain place in book.*) Ah, here it is. We'll jump in right here where the Royal Wise Person arrives. (*Returns to chair.*)

STAGEHAND. Cue the Royal Wise Person! (*Disappears behind curtain.*)

THE LADY. Oh, I do like the Royal Wise Person. She always wears such wonderful hats. (*Reading.*) And as the last of the pythons swallowed a small, slow member of the audience, the Queen said, "Oh, I do wish ..." (*QUEEN takes over the line on "do" and THE LADY lets go of the line on "do". CAST unfreezes on the word "do"—brushes off their clothes, straighten hats, etc.*)

QUEEN. Oh, I do wish the Royal Wise Person were here. She always knows just what to do.

ROYAL WISE PERSON. (*Enters from Stage Left. Stands just to left of LADY 6. Is rather bored.*) Your Highness requests my presence? (*THE LADY turns and sees ROYAL WISE PERSON's hat, gasps, stares enraptured.*)

QUEEN. Oh, Royal Wise Person, there you are. What luck! How do you do that?

ROYAL WISE PERSON.   Your wish is my command, remember?

QUEEN. Oh yes, of course, that's so convenient. Well, let me explain all this to you. I know it looks like a game but it's not.

ROYAL WISE PERSON. Your Highness ...

QUEEN. I know. I was disappointed, too, but this is a very serious situation ...

ROYAL WISE PERSON. Not necessary, Your Highness. I have the whole picture. I'm the Royal Wise Person, remember?

QUEEN. Oh yes, of course you are. So, what should we do?

ROYAL WISE PERSON. (*With a shrug.*) Easy. A princess test. (*CAST ad libs excited comments about having a princess test.*)

ROYAL WISE PERSON. Ahem! (*CAST is immediately silent.*) Whoever loses is not a princess and, therefore, must go back the way she came and let the other one pass. (*To TWINKLEBERRY.*) Agreed?

TWINKLEBERRY. Agreed. (*Very excited.*) Oh, I'm good at princess tests. I learned all about them at princess school.

ROYAL WISE PERSON. (*To POPPLEPEA.*) Agreed?

POPPLEPEA. Agreed. (*ROYAL WISE PERSON passes down two pencils and two pieces of paper. CAST passes them from hand to hand in a uniform, synchronized manner.*)

TWINKLEBERRY. You didn't go to princess school, did you?

POPPLEPEA. No.

TWINKLEBERRY. Oh goody.

POPPLEPEA. I've read a lot of books though.

TWINKLEBERRY. Books! Huh! What good are they? I never read books.

POPPLEPEA. (*A little smile.*) Oh goody. (*By now both princesses have their paper and pencil. TWINKLEBEERY has refused to hand POPPLEPEA hers so ROYAL GUARD 1 hands them over.*)

QUEEN. Well, what will it be? A pop quiz? Multiple-choice? An essay? (*CAST makes a little groaning noise at suggestion of an essay.*)

ROYAL WISE PERSON. No, no. I'm not in an academic mood. I think — a riddle. (*CAST ad libs general excitement over it being a riddle.*)

ROYAL WISE PERSON. Ahem! (*CAST is immediately silent.*) And the riddle is: What is as large as the sky, as round as the earth and as thin ... (*Picks thread off her dress, drops it over cliff and CAST watches as it falls to the ground.*) as a thread?

CAST. (*Thinking very hard.*) Hhhmmmmmmmmmmmm.

TWINKLEBERRY. I got it! I got it! (*Writing, terribly pleased with herself,*) I got it, I got it, I got it, I got it, I got it! (*Passes paper left. POPPLEPEA calmly writes, passes paper left. This time TWINKLEBERRY tries to take it but POPPLEPEA hands it to ROYAL GUARD 1. CAST again passes down the papers in a uniform, synchronized manner.*)

ROYAL WISE PERSON. And to repeat the riddle one last time: What is as large as the sky, as round as the earth and as thin as a thread? And Twinkleberry's answer is ... (*LADY 6 hands her the paper, ROYAL WISE PERSON opens it, CAST watches eagerly.*) the horizon.

CAST. Ahhhh!

ROYAL WISE PERSON. Which is — correct. (*CAST applauds, looking down at TWINKLEBERRY who is bowing, preening, eating it up.*)

ROYAL WISE PERSON. And Popplepea's answer is ... (*LADY 6 hands her the paper. ROYAL WISE PERSON opens it, CAST watches eagerly. ROYAL WISE PERSON reads it with puzzlement.*) an egg?

CAST. (*With puzzlement, looking down at POPPLEPEA.*)

An egg?

POPPLEPEA. (*With perfect composure.*) Of course an egg. An egg is the sky to the chick inside it. As for being round as the earth, the earth isn't round. It's slightly oval ... (*Holding up egg.*) like an egg. (*To TWINKLEBERRY.*) I read that in a book.

TWINKLEBERRY. (*Sarcastically.*) And I suppose an egg is as thin as a thread?

POPPLEPEA. (*Takes needle from collar.*) Here. Take my needle. (*TWINKLEBERRY does.*) Now hold it up — just so. Look through it's eye. (*TWINKLEBERRY does. POPPLEPEA holds egg out in front of TWINKLEBERRY.*) Can you see the egg?

TWINKLEBERRY. (*Bored.*) Yes.

POPPLEPEA. All of it?

TWINKLEBERRY. Not quite.

POPPLEPEA. (*Moves egg a little further away.*) Now?

TWINKLEBERRY. Yes.

POPPLEPEA. You can see all the egg?

TWINKLEBERRY. (*With growing impatience.*) Yes!

POPPLEPEA. You can see the entire egg through the eye of this needle?

TWINKLEBERRY. Yes!

POPPLEPEA. (*Casually.*) What else fits through the eye of a needle?

TWINKLEBERRY. (*Without thinking.*) A thread! (*Realizes what she's said. Gasps.*)

CAST. (*Really impressed. Turns back to ROYAL WISE PERSON.*) Aaaaaaahhhhhhhhh!!!!!

ROYAL WISE PERSON. (*Hadn't expected this. Is really having to think.*) Also ... correct. (*CAST turns back to POPPLEPEA, applauding with much more enthusiasm than last time.*)

TWINKLEBERRY. No! No! There can only be one correct answer! And I had it! I had it! She cheated! It isn't fair!

QUEEN. Oh, do be quiet, dear.

ROYAL WISE PERSON. Of course there can be more than one correct answer. There can be as many correct answers as there are clever people. (*Leans forward, speaks to POPPLEPEA with sincerity.*) You are a very clever person, indeed.

POPPLEPEA. Thank you.

ROYAL WISE PERSON. You're welcome.

TWINKLEBERRY. But who won? Somebody must have won?

QUEEN. Oh yes, who won? We really must get off this mountain. I can't face another rock slide.

ROYAL WISE PERSON. (*Thinking hard.*) Well, this has never happened before. One is always an imposter. But they both passed the test which means they're both princesses which means ... (*A blank look.*) I don't know what that means.

QUEEN. (*Horrified.*) Oh dear.

ROYAL WISE PERSON. (*With growing alarm.*) This has never happened before. I don't know something!

QUEEN. Oh dear, oh dear. What's to be done?

ROYAL WISE PERSON. (*Close to panic.*) I don't know!

QUEEN. You said it again!

ROYAL WISE PERSON. I know! (*Thinking hard, rubbing temples. CAST is silently urging her on.*) Oh, wait wait — I think I'm getting something. Yes, yes — it's getting clearer. Of course! It's obvious! We'll have to change the law of the land! (*CAST looks relieved.*)

QUEEN. Thank goodness. (*But then another cause for alarm.*) But how long will that take?

ROYAL WISE PERSON. I don't know. (*CAST once again looks worried.*)

QUEEN. Oh!

ROYAL WISE PERSON. But I'll find out! I'll go back to the castle. I'll talk to the Royal Lawyers and the Royal Barristers ...

POPPLEPEA. No, no. That won't be necessary. I'll be very glad to step aside so that anyone who cares to, may pass. (*Walks to far Stage Right.*)

TWINKLEBERRY. Well, it is about time! I have never been so inconvenienced in all my life! Wait till Daddy hears about this!

QUEEN. Twinkleberry! (*Very weary.*) Just go, Twinkleberry! (*TWINKLEBERRY exits in a huff, giving a toss of her head as she walks by POPPLEPEA. ROYAL GUARD are hurrying along right behind her.*)

ROYAL GUARD 1. Sorry about that thing with the handcuffs. (*Exits.*)

ROYAL GUARD 2. Lovely meeting you. (*Exits.*)

ROYAL GUARD 3. Good luck with your egg. (*Exits.*)

SOLDIER 1. (*To GENERAL.*) Do we still get to charge?

GENERAL. (*To QUEEN.*) Would it be all right, Your Majesty? They have their hearts set on it.

QUEEN. Oh, maybe just a little. Charge, but don't kill anybody.

GENERAL. We get to charge! (*Great cheering and excitement.*) Men! Brandish arms! (*Draw swords.*) CHAAAAARRRRGGEE!!!!!!! (*GENERAL and SOLDIERS charge Offstage Right yelling and waving swords and making a great spectacle. We hear the noise continue as they zigzag around the stage behind the scenery a few times and then they finally fade away.*)

QUEEN. (*Walking to Stage Right. LADIES follow her.*) Good luck to you, my dear.

POPPLEPEA. (*A curtsey.*) Thank you, Your Majesty.

QUEEN.   Come along, Ladies.   (*Thinks of something. Pauses by POPPLEPEA for a moment. Speaks confidentially.*) If you ever have a need for any Ladies-in-Waiting, let me know. (*Exits.*)

LADY 1. (*LADIES speak with growing alarm and sniffles.*) What did she mean by that? (*Exits.*)

LADY 2. It means she wants to get rid of us. (*Exits.*)

LADY 3. Get rid of us? (*Exits.*)

LADY 4. All of us? (*Exits.*)

LADY 5. But why would she want to do that? (*Exits.*)

LADY 6. (*Bawling.*) We're so much fun! (*Exits sobbing and we hear all the other LADIES back there sobbing louder than ever.*)

ROYAL WISE PERSON. (*Still at far Stage Left.   Tone is curious but respectful.*) Why did you do that? You didn't have to.

POPPLEPEA. (*Calm, regal.*) Of course I didn't have to. I chose to. And now I must get to market to sell my egg, so if you care to pass ... (*Gesturing right.*)

ROYAL WISE PERSON. Oh no. Please — allow me, (*Curtsies very low and holds it.*) Your Majesty. (*Bows head.*)

POPPLEPEA. (*Walks calmly and regally across stage. When she gets to ROYAL WISE PERSON she pauses.*) Up, up. (*ROYAL WISE PERSON stands. POPPLEPEA smiles and exits.*)

ROYAL WISE PERSON. (*Walking toward Center Stage, glancing back at where POPPLEPEA exited.*) There goes a real princess.

THE LADY. (*Closes book, stands. STAGEHAND has come out with small stepladder which she sets up so ROYAL WISE PERSON can come down Offstage. Then STAGEHAND exits with ladder.*) And, as usual, the Royal Wise Person was right. Because, as everyone knows, it isn't the clothes or the hair or the perfume or the powder that make a princess.

ROYAL WISE PERSON. (*Is now standing next to THE LADY.*) Oh no.

THE LADY. It's the kindness and good manners and good sense and generosity that make a princess — (*With sincerity.*) and all of the rest of us — real.

ROYAL WISE PERSON. From then on Twinkleberry was very careful never to leave late ...

THE LADY. And Popplepea was very careful never to leave early, so they never met again. But I have it on very good authority ...

ROYAL WISE PERSON. I told her.

THE LADY. That Popplepea ... (*THE LADY and ROYAL WISE PERSON look fondly over their shoulders after POPPLEPEA, then back at the audience.*) lived happily ever after. (*A definite change in tone and expression from pleasant to unpleasant.*) And Twinkleberry ... (*A frown over their shoulders after TWINKLEBERRY, then back to the audience. THE LADY says this with great satisfaction.*) didn't.

(*MUSIC begins. THE LADY and ROYAL WISE PERSON curtsy low and hold it while CAST, led by STAGEHAND, come out from Stage Left in the same order as during the performance. Women curtsey. Men bow from the waist.*)

THE END

COSTUMES

THE LADY WHO TELLS THE STORY: Layers of eccentric clothing — ruffly blouse, little jacket, petticoats, skirt, apron, sweatpants, bright sox, canvas shoes. This should be bright, cheerful, mismatched, decidedly feminine clothing. Nothing ugly, dirty or torn. An elaborate hat.

TWINKLEBERRY: A beautiful gown, jewelry, tiara, gloves, cape — the works.

POPPLEPEA: A simple, flowered, floor-length cotton dress with a sash.

ROYAL GUARD: Brightly colored tunics over turtlenecks and leotards. Matching headgear and spears.

GENERAL GOOGE AND SOLDIERS: Black jeans, belts, baseball caps and high-tops. Gray tunics over gray sweatshirts. The General's uniform should also have gold cording looped at the shoulders and across chest, stripe going up side of pants, "shiny stuff" (gold foil fringe) at shoulders and on cap. They all carry swords.

QUEEN: A gold crown. An elegant dress, elegant jewelry.

LADIES-IN-WAITING: Long gowns with filmy overskirts, cone hats with filmy fabric hanging down from peak, lots of ribbons and bows everywhere.

STAGEHAND: Jeans, baggy shirt or sweatshirt, tennis shoes.

ROYAL WISE PERSON: Simple, black, floor-length dress. A hat even more elaborate than The Lady Who Tells The Story's hat.

PROPS

THE LADY WHO TELLS THE STORY: An old push, non-power lawnmower. A big purse containing a large, lacey hanky, food (a pickle, a sandwich, etc.) a storybook entitled"The Princess And The Princess."

TWINKLEBERRY: A pretty hand mirror.

POPPLEPEA: A worn-out looking evening gown, a basket, a large white plastic egg, a fairly large needle slipped into collar of her dress.

ROYAL GUARD 1: A set of handcuffs.

ROYAL WISE PERSON: Two small pencils, two small pieces of paper.

STAGEHAND: A sandwich. A small stepladder.

TWICE UPON A TIME
Flexible cast of 20
One simple set
25 minute playing time

Twice Upon a Time was first performed by the Greenleaf 4-H Club in Green Bay, WI on November 7, 1987 with the following cast:

STORYTELLER	Dawn Gibson
FERMELDA	Megan Neuman
SLUG	Max Neuman
GRUB	Maggy Clancy
CINDERELLA	Jenny Pleshek
SLEEPING BEAUTY	Shelly Pleshek
SNOW WHITE	Patty Clancy
ALLERGIC	Barbie Pleshek
SARCASTIC	Sonya Blaese
STUPID	Toni Maufort
DEPRESSED	Rikki Garrity
BORED	Ginelle Gilson
JUST PLAIN MEAN	Heather Clancy
EXHAUSTED	Kristen Neuman
BEAUTY	Michelle Vista
PRINCESS AND THE PEA	Tania Blaese
ABRA	Shannon Koomen
CA	Courtney Guyette
DABRA	Michelle Gibson
FROG	Katie Clancy

CHARACTERS

STORYTELLER
FERMELDA
SLUG
GRUB
CINDERELLA
SLEEPING BEAUTY
SNOW WHITE
ALLERGIC
SARCASTIC
STUPID
DEPRESSED
BORED
JUST PLAIN MEAN
EXHAUSTED
BEAUTY
PRINCESS AND THE PEA
ABRA
CA
DABRA
FROG

Note: The number of Dwarfs and Soldiers (the Abra, Ca and Dabra characters) is flexible. For Dwarfs, just redistribute the lines to accommodate more or fewer performers. The Soldiers don't have lines so you may use as many as you like. There must be a minimum of three Soldiers to respond to the names Abra, Ca and Dabra.

TWICE UPON A TIME

*(The play takes place in a witches' cave. There is a
large, black witches' pot at Center Stage with three long
sticks in it for stirring and three old stools or boxes
arranged around it for the witches to sit on. There are
more stools and boxes scattered around the stage for the
princesses to sit on. At Center Stage there is a small
raggy rug under which there is a large flat book. A
shelf behind the pot has a bottle of floor wax, a jar of
bat's eyes, a large bottle of muddy water and three old
bowls or cups. A backdrop of webbing with spiders,
bats, skulls, etc, is optional.)*

STORYTELLER. *(Enters from behind closed curtain and
stands Center Stage. Holding an open storybook.)*
In Storyland we have some rules.
If there are swords, there must be duels.
The frog, if there is one, must be green.
And the giants, when there are some, have to be mean.
And witches, of course, wear black hats and hiss.
And the prince and the princess? They have to kiss.
But before any of that, I have to say
"Once Upon A Time."
It's always been that way.

*(CURTAIN starts to open. FERMELDA, GRUB and
SLUG are seated around pot, stirring with sticks.)*

But when their book got lost
Their spells got crossed
And the witches — all three —

Are as mad as can be.
So today,
They say,
I have to end my rhyme
With not just once,
But twice upon a time. (*Exits.*)

FERMELDA. Double, double, toil and trouble. Fire burn and cauldron bubble. (*All three lean forward and look hopefully into pot. Lean back, disappointed. Sigh, keep stirring.*)

SLUG. I think that I shall never see a poem lovely as a tree. (*All three lean forward and look hopefully into pot. Lean back, disappointed. Sigh, keep stirring.*)

GRUB. Four score and seven years ago. (*All three lean forward, look hopefully into pot. Lean back, disappointed. Sigh, keep stirring.*)

FERMELDA. (*To GRUB.*) Four score and seven years ago? (*To SLUG.*) Poems about trees? (*Slumps back and looks discouraged.*) We don't even sound like witches anymore. We sound like poets. And politicians. I hate this.

SLUG. You hate this? What about me? I hate this! And it's all your fault, Grub!

GRUB. My fault? My fault?! You're the one who lost the book! This is your fault, Slug! (*GRUB and SLUG are glaring at each other over the pot and now slowly rise as they yell at each other.*)

SLUG. Me? Me?! I didn't lose the book! You lost the book! I saw you with it last!

GRUB. Liar! Liar! I never touched the book! I never even saw the book! I'm innocent! Innocent! Innocent!

FERMELDA. Knock it off! (*They sit down but continue to hiss at each other. To SLUG.*) Put in some more bat's eyes.

SLUG. (*Reaches over to shelf behind her, takes something*

out of a bottle and throws into pot.) Oooh, I love it when they stick to my fingers. (*Licks fingers.*)

FERMELDA. (*Leans ahead and looks in pot.*) Nothing. (*Stops stirring.*) That's it. I've had it. I quit! (*Tosses stick into pot. Stands up and begins pacing back and forth.*) We've been stirring this sludge for three weeks! We've done incantations, chants, voodoo, black magic, blue magic, black and blue magic and it still isn't right! (*Stops at pot and looks into it.*) It isn't green. It doesn't have lumps. There's no oil slick on top. I hate this. I can't stand it anymore. (*Slumps back down into chair.*)

GRUB. But you're head witch, Fermelda. You're supposed to know this stuff.

FERMELDA. (*Jumps back up in frustration.*) I told you! I've tried everything! Poached monkey's eyes! Buffalo warts! Oil of kangaroo pouch! Scrambled eggs and catsup! Nothing works! (*Sarcastically.*) What do you want me to do? Say Abracadabra?! (*CINDERELLA enters Stage Right as though blown in by a wind. She staggers around a bit, getting her balance. The WITCHES, startled by her appearance, scoot away to Stage Left. CINDERELLA gets her bearings, sees the WITCHES and gives a little screech of surprise. This causes the WITCHES to give their own little screech of surprise.*)

CINDERELLA. Oooh! My! You're unpleasant looking!

GRUB. (*Thinks this is a compliment. Pats hair.*) Why, thank you.

FERMELDA. (*Not so friendly.*) Who are you, girlie?

SLUG. (*Very unfriendly.*) And what are you doing in our cave?

CINDERELLA. Why, I'm Cinderella. And I'm on my way to the ball. So (*Flounces skirt, strikes her prettiest pose.*) where's the prince? She said there'd be a prince.

SLUG. Boy, are you in the wrong cave!

GRUB. There's no ball here, dearie.

FERMELDA. No princes either. (*The WITCHES have come a little closer.*) Say, you know anything about spells?

CINDERELLA. Oh yes. I was the best speller in the third grade. Why, I could even spell Mississippi backwards. Let's see — I, P, P, I ...

FERMELDA. No, no, no! Not spelling. Spells. You know — magic. Hocuspocus. Witch stuff!

CINDERELLA. Oh. Well, I wouldn't know about that. You see, I am a princess. Though up until tonight I've had to live like a scullery maid. I don't mind telling you it's been dreadful. But that's all over now. Tonight is my night. So, if you don't mind, I really must be going. (*Looks expectantly at WITCHES. They stare blankly back at her.*) Go ahead. Whisk me away. (*She waits and they stare again.*) I don't think you understand. This is my only chance. If I don't show up at that ball tonight, it will be cinders and floor wax for the rest of my life.

SLUG. Cinders!

GRUB. Floor wax! (*They run back to pot. SLUG scrapes up cinders from around pot and throws them in. GRUB grabs bottle of floor wax off shelf and throws it in. They stir hopefully.*)

FERMELDA. (*Glances into pot without much hope and then turns back to CINDERELLA.*) Well, you're out of luck, girlie.

CINDERELLA. What do you mean?

FERMELDA. (*Shrugs.*) We don't know how you got here. And if we don't know how you got here, we can't send you back.

CINDERELLA. What do you mean you don't know how I got here?

FERMELDA. (*Shrugs again.*) All I said was Abracadabra! (*SLEEPING BEAUTY comes staggering out Stage Left. The WITCHES and CINDERELLA scurry away to Stage Right.*)

SLEEPING BEAUTY. (*Yawning, rubbing eyes.*) So, what time

is it? I didn't hear the alarm. (*Sees WITCHES.*) Oh no. I've got to stop eating clam dip at bedtime. I'm having another nightmare.

SLUG. (*Insulted.*) I'm no nightmare! I'm a witch. And I'm real. Name's Slug. And (*Looking her up and down, sarcastically.*) let me guess. I'll bet you're a princess.

SLEEPING BEAUTY. That's right. Of course I am. See the crown? But I don't have a name. Everyone just calls me Sleeping Beauty. I've always wanted a real name — like Roxanne or maybe Mimi. (*Yawns, looks around.*) So, where's the prince? If he'd give me kiss, maybe I could wake up a little here. I could die for a nap. (*WITCHES shake their heads in disgust, return to pot.*)

CINDERELLA. (*Coming closer.*) Excuse me. There isn't any prince. But if there was one, he'd be mine.

SLEEPING BEAUTY. I don't think so. I'm Sleeping Beauty. I get the prince. Don't you ever read?

CINDERELLA. I'm Cinderella. I get the prince. Don't you ever go to the movies?

FERMELDA. Enough! Sit down and be quiet! I need to think! (*PRINCESSES sit on some boxes, Stage Right, near GRUB. They continue to glare at each other.*)

GRUB. Well, this is so nice. It's been so long since we've had company. Could I get you something to drink? We have some nice brown water. (*Offers jar of brown water.*)

CINDERELLA. Oh, how nice. Tea?

GRUB. (*Confused.*) No. Just brown water. (*CINDERELLA looks repulsed.*)

SLUG. Give me that! (*Grabs jar.*) What are you doing? They're not company. They're princesses — yukky, ikky, gooey, gummy princesses. They didn't come here for a cozy little visit. They landed here. By accident.

SLEEPING BEAUTY. We did?
GRUB. (*Still being pleasant.*) Oh yes. You see, all she said (*Points to FERMELDA.*) was Abracadabra!

(*FERMELDA and SLUG gasp and say "No!" but it's too late. SNOW WHITE and the seven DWARFS come whirling out Stage Right and whirl all across to Stage Left where SNOW WHITE finally stops and the DWARFS all land in a heap.*)

FERMELDA. (*Coming forward, no longer surprised by these appearances.*) Well, well. What a surprise. A princess. Now, who might you be? (*Looking at DWARFS.*) As if I didn't know.
SNOW WHITE. (*Extremely sweet with a trace of Southern accent.*) Why, I'm Snow White. And these are my seven little friends. Go ahead — introduce yourselves. (*The DWARFS have stood up and now arrange themselves in a line with ALLERGIC next to SNOW WHITE and ending with EXHAUSTED directly in front of the witches' pot.*)
ALLERGIC. I'm Allergic. (*Sneezes.*)
SARCASTIC. (*With a sneer.*) I'm Sarcastic.
STUPID. (*With very blank expression.*) I'm Stupid.
DEPRESSED. (*Dismally.*) I'm Depressed.
BORED. (*Whining.*) I'm Bored.
JUST PLAIN MEAN. (*Snarling.*) I'm Just Plain Mean.
EXHAUSTED. And I'm Exhausted. (*Yawns.*)
SLEEPING BEAUTY. (*Catching the yawn.*) Me too. (*Yawns another enormous yawn and begins to fall asleep.*)
SNOW WHITE. They're the Seven Dwarfs. And we all live together ...
GRUB AND SLUG. Dwarfs! (*Grab EXHAUSTED and try to put him in the pot. SNOW WHITE comes to his rescue, yanks*

*him away. EXHAUSTED and the other DWARFS cower behind
SNOW WHITE.)*

SNOW WHITE. How dare you! What a way to behave!

SLUG. How do you expect us to behave? We're witches.

SNOW WHITE. That's no excuse. Why, when my prince
comes, he'll teach you a thing or two. (*Looks around.*) He is
coming, isn't he? (*WITCHES cackle, return to pot.*)

CINDERELLA. (*Crooks finger at SNOW WHITE.*) Hey.
You. Over here. (*SNOW WHITE comes closer, DWARFS stay
right behind her.*) Let me explain something to you. I'm
Cinderella ...

SNOW WHITE. (*Still being extremely sweet.*) Oh, how do
you do?

CINDERELLA. Very well, thank you. There's something
you should understand here ...

SNOW WHITE. And I'm Snow White.

CINDERELLA. So I heard. The thing is ...

SNOW WHITE. Lovely to meet you.

CINDERELLA. You want to hear this or not?

SNOW WHITE. Well, I'd just love to.

CINDERELLA. Well, like I said, I'm Cinderella and this over
here, this is Sleeping Beauty (*They look over and SLEEPING
BEAUTY is sound asleep. She snores one loud snore and her
head flops over.*) and we're both here because of some stupid
mix-up (*Shoots the WITCHES a nasty look. They hiss back at
her.*) BUT if and when the prince shows up, he's mine.

SNOW WHITE. Well, I do beg to differ, dear, but the prince
is, in fact, mine. All mine. Why I had to flee to the forest for
my very life! I've had to clean a filthy cottage and cook for
seven — that is seven — little men who for the size of them could
eat a buffalo apiece a day! I haven't gone through all this for
nothing! That prince has my name on him, sister! (*Clears

throat, gets back sweet voice.) I mean, dear.

CINDERELLA. (*Paces as she speaks and when she gets close to SNOW WHITE she leans straight into her face, causing SNOW WHITE and the seven DWARFS, who are still right behind her, to lean backwards.*) You think you've had it rough? You ever wax a marble staircase? Our castle has nineteen of them! Forty-seven bedrooms that castle has, one hundred and seventy-six windows and that's not counting storms and screens! And at least those little guys appreciate you. (*DWARFS look at audience and shake their heads.*) With my stepmother and stepsisters it's pick, pick, pick — nag, nag, nag. Nothing is ever good enough for them — the three old ... (*Looks over at WITCHES who hiss and give her hex signs.*) I knew they reminded me of somebody.

FERMELDA. (*Jumps up and comes forward.*) Enough! Enough of this bickering! Who cares about your stupid lives! My head is splitting! And, so help me, if I never hear the word Abracadabra again it will be too soon! (*Realizes what she's said, gasps and clasps hands over mouth but it's too late. BEAUTY enters in a whirlwind Stage Right. SNOW WHITE and DWARFS scoot back to Stage Left.*)

BEAUTY. Oh my! Thank goodness! I'm finally out of there! (*Clutching at FERMELDA.*) There isn't a Beast in here, is there?

FERMELDA. No! There isn't a Beast in here! You didn't bring one with you, did you?

BEAUTY. (*Looking fearfully around.*) I hope not!

FERMELDA. Because this cave is already so full of princesses I can hardly turn around! (*Turns around and bumps into CINDERELLA.*) Oh! My head!

GRUB. Here, Fermelda. Put a rock on it. (*Offers rock which FERMELDA takes, puts on head, sighs in relief.*)

BEAUTY. Well, you don't have to worry about me. I'm not a princess. I'm just an incredibly good-looking commoner.

CINDERELLA. Really?

BEAUTY. Well, my name is Beauty, after all. And I won't complain about being here. I like it here. I may never leave. (*FERMELDA groans even louder. GRUB and SLUG pat her comfortingly on the back.*)

SNOW WHITE. Well, I'm just curious — why would anyone want to stay in a nasty, damp cave full of spiders ... (*Stamps on a spider.*) and witches? There's nothing worse than spiders ... (*Stamps on another one.*) and witches do lack a certain charm.

BEAUTY. You haven't seen the Beast. He's twelve feet tall, covered with filthy black hair, has squinty little yellow eyes, hundreds of rotten brown teeth, b-a-a-a-d breath and no table manners to speak of.

SNOW WHITE. My, that does sound unpleasant. But just remember if a prince shows up, keep your hands to yourself. He's mine.

CINDERELLA. I was here first! He's mine!

SNOW WHITE. No one cares if you were here first!

CINDERELLA. First come, first serve!

BEAUTY. (*Very interested.*) There's a prince? Coming here?

CINDERELLA. Forget about it. You said it yourself — you're a commoner.

BEAUTY. (*Using compact to touch up makeup.*) I'm a commoner — with potential.

SNOW WHITE. (*To CINDERELLA.*) Now see what you started!

CINDERELLA. Me? You had to start talking about princes ...

FERMELDA. (*Jumping up.*) Stop it! Stop it, stop it, stop it, stop it, stop it! One more word out of any of you and I'll turn you all into toads!

GRUB. (*Standing up.*) Don't be silly, Fermelda. We can't turn anybody into anything. Nothing works. We've been trying for weeks and weeks and nothing works. Nothing, that is, except Abraca … ! (*FERMELDA and SLUG clap their hands over her mouth. EVERYONE looks around, holding their breath. Nothing happens. They let go of her, sighing in relief.*)

BEAUTY. Well, why don't you say it right? Even I know it's Abracadabra! (*EVERYONE gasps, "No!" but again it's too late. PRINCESS/PEA marches out Stage Right followed by her SOLDIERS carrying the mattress.*)

PRINCESS/PEA. (*Walks and talks like a drill sergeant.*) And … HALT! (*SOLDIERS halt at Center Stage.*) All right. Here we are. The royal bedchamber. And it's about time too. LOWER MATTRESS! (*They lower it directly on to the small rug.*) Straighten it up there, straighten it up! (*They do.*) FALL IN! (*They form line Stage Right.*) ABOUT FACE! (*They do.*) FORWARD MARCH! (*They only go about a half-step when FERMELDA stops them.*)

FERMELDA. Hold it right there! (*To PRINCESS/PEA.*) They're not going anywhere. Who are you, anyway?

PRINCESS/PEA. (*Incensed.*) Me? Why, I'm the princess!

FERMELDA. Oh yeah? You and everybody else in this dump. Which princess?

PRINCESS/PEA. I am the princess! Of the Princess and The Pea. Here are my peas (*Holds up large can of peas.*) and these are my faithful servants. BOW! (*They are still facing away from her and they start bowing. Since she neglects to tell them to stop bowing, they just keep on bowing.*) See? And they're going to get the rest of my twenty-seven mattresses!

SLEEPING BEAUTY. (*Woke up when PRINCESS/PEA and*

SOLDIERS came marching on. She now comes closer.) You have twenty-seven mattresses?

PRINCESS/PEA. I got twenty-seven mattresses! Top of the line — everyone of them! Best mattresses you can get! I got firm, extra firm, soft, squishy. I got duck feathers, chicken feathers, goose feathers, straw! I got 'em all!

SLEEPING BEAUTY. Well, then, I'm sure you wouldn't mind if I just took one teensy weensy little nap on this one. (*Starts to step on to mattress.*)

PRINCESS/PEA. Take one step closer to this mattress and ... (*Finally notices where she is.*) Say, what is this place?

SLEEPING BEAUTY. (*Somewhat impatiently. She's thinking about the mattress.*) This is the witches' cave and this is Cinderella and this is Snow White and those are the seven dwarves and that is Beauty Somebody-or-other and I'm Sleeping Beauty and we're all here because someone keeps saying (*EVERYONE gasps. She catches herself in time.*) the "A" word and all I want to do is take one teensy weensy little nap ...

PRINCESSS/PEA. Never mind all that. Where's the prince?

EVERYONE. (*Except SOLDIERS.*) There isn't any prince!

PRINCESS/PEA. No prince?

EVERYONE. (*Except SOLDIERS.*) No prince!

PRINCESS/PEA. Men! FORWARD MARCH! (*SOLDIERS start to march forward but they're still bowing.*) STOP THAT BOWING! Turn around and get back here! Pick up this mattress! We're gettin' outta here!

SLEEPING BEAUTY. (*Stops SOLDIERS by jumping on mattress, landing in sitting position.*) What are you doing? Where are you taking it?

PRINCESS/PEA.   I'm not hanging around a damp old cave full of witches and a bunch of second-rate so-called princesses! I got me a prince to find!

SLEEPING BEAUTY. Well, you can't leave.
PRINCESS/PEA. Says who?
SLEEPING BEAUTY. No one can. You're stuck here. Just like us.
PRINCESS/PEA. We'll see about that. I'm calling my men over here, they're picking up this mattress and nobody's going to stop us. Abra! (*First SOLDIER steps forward and salutes. EVERYONE gasps a little.*) Ca! (*Second SOLDIER does same. EVERYONE gasps a little more.*) Dabra! (*Third SOLDIER does same. EVERYONE gasps "No!" but it's too late. This time a FROG comes whirling out from Stage Left.*)
FROG. (*Very confused.*) Ribet! (*Even more confused.*) Ribet, ribet, ribet, ribet! (*Astonished that he can't speak English. Notices his hands and stares at them. Even more upset.*) Ribet, ribet, ribet, ribet ... !
FERMELDA. Oh good. Princesses weren't bad enough. Now we're getting frogs. (*Pauses for a moment, noticing how upset the FROG is.*) What's the matter with him?
GRUB. Oh, he says he can't understand why he keeps saying "ribet" or how he got all green and slimy. I used to be a frog. I speak the language.
FERMELDA. Well, tell him to calm down. My head is bursting.
GRUB. (*Calm and reassuring.*) Ribet, ribet, ribet, ribet, ribet. (*FROG relieved someone understands him, tells his story with lots of "ribets" and gestures. GRUB nods and listens.*) Uh-huh, uh-huh. Okay. Yes I see, I see. Well, well, well. (*To others.*) He says he used to be a ... (*Realizes this could start a riot. Whispers it to FERMELDA and SLUG. CINDERELLA leans in and hears it too.*)
CINDERELLA. A prince! A prince! He used to be a prince!
SNOW WHITE. He's mine! (*Grabs FROG's arm.*)

CINDERELLA. Let go of him! I saw him first! (*Grabs FROG's other arm.*)

BEAUTY. (*Checking makeup.*) He's a frog with potential.

PRINCESS/PEA.   Listen, pal, I'm the only real princess around here. See? I'm the only one with a can of peas.

CINDERELLA.   (*To WITCHES.*)   Turn him back! (*EVERYONE begins yelling for the WITCHES to turn the FROG back. SLEEPING BEAUTY sees her chance and lays down on the mattress, curls up and goes to sleep.*)

FERMELDA. Stop it! Stop, stop, stop, stop, stop it! (*No one is paying any attention to her. Jumps up on box.*) We can't turn him back! We've lost our powers! (*This gets their attention.*) Don't you see? That's what this is all about! We didn't bring you here on purpose! Or him either! We can't conjure up anything or conjure down anything! We're witches in name only. (*Steps down off box in dejection.*)

SLUG. Because Grub lost the book.

GRUB. Because Slug lost the book.

FERMELDA. It doesn't matter who lost the book! All that matters is that it's gone. And we're nothing without it. Pretty soon we're going to have to start wearing regular clothes. (*WITCHES shudder.*) Live in a house. (*Shudder again.*) Get jobs. (*They really shudder this time. FERMELDA sits down.*)

CINDERELLA. Book?

SNOW WHITE. What book?

FERMELDA.   The recipe book.You don't think we can remember all that witch stuff, do you? Why, there must be seven thousand spells on toad transformations alone! So we wrote it down. In the book.

SLUG. And we only had one copy.

FERMELDA. And it's gone.

FERMELADA, SLUG AND GRUB. Gone, gone, gone, gone,

gone.   (*They slump over in defeat.   Their depression is contagious.   One by one, the PRINCESSES give up.*)

SNOW WHITE.   Well, I guess that means no prince. (*Drops FROG's arm and sits down.*)

CINDERELLA.   I guess I won't be going dancing tonight. (*Sits down.*) Or ever. (*Buries face in hands.*)

BEAUTY.   I look gorgeous for absolutely nothing. Again. (*Sits down.*)

PRINCESS/PEA.   Might as well eat my peas.   (*Pulls can opener out of pocket.*)

SLEEPING BEAUTY.   (*Has been tossing and turning during last few speeches.   Now in great agitation she sits up and begins rummaging around under mattress.   Yanks out book.*) Ah ha! A stupid book! No wonder I couldn't sleep! (*She prepares to throw book out into audience.   EVERYONE's heads pop up at the word "book."*)

CINDERELLA. Book?

SNOW WHITE. Book?

BEAUTY. Book?

PRINCESS/PEA. Did she say book?

FERMELDA. (*Coming forward.*) Our book! (*Grabs it before SLEEPING BEAUTY can throw it.*)   It's our book!   Our beautiful, fabulous, magnificent book! (*Three WITCHES are ecstatic, cackling, dancing, hugging the book.*)

CINDERELLA. Well, it is about time.

SNOW WHITE. I'll say. Let's go.

BEAUTY. (*Looking alarmed.*) Time for what? Go where?

PRINCESS/PEA. Stop that jumpin' around, you three, and get us outta here! I got a prince waitin' for me! Send us back!

FERMELDA.   (*Gleefully.*) Send you back? I'll send you back! I'll send you back so fast your heads will spin! And don't think I won't be glad to get rid of the lot of you! If I never see

another diamond tiara it will be too soon! (*Gets up on box directly behind pot, opens book.*) Ah, here it is, here it is. (*With big gestures and great drama.*)
Lightning, stars and rolling thunder!
Lizards, moles and things down under!
Light the sky with fire and ice!
Make them disappear — once, twice, thrice! (*WITCHES look expectantly at PRINCESSES who look expectantly back at them. Nothing happens. BEAUTY looks relieved. Then, surprising everyone, the FROG speaks.*)

FROG. (*Steps forward. Clears throat.*) Well, that's better. I thought I'd never speak again.

CINDERELLA. Ribet! (*Gasps and clasps hands over mouth.*)

SNOW WHITE. (*Finds this amusing.*) Ribet! (*Gasps and clasps hands over mouth.*)

SLEEPING BEAUTY. (*With a yawn.*) Ribet! (*Almost looks awake.*)

BEAUTY. (*Cautiously.*) Ribet? (*Looks distraught.*)

PRINCESS/PEA. (*An order.*) Ribet! (*Looks furious.*)

DWARFS AND SOLDIERS. (*Look at audience and say in unison.*) Ribet!

FERMELDA. No! No, no, no! They're supposed to disappear!

SLUG. (*Gets up on box and grabs book.*) Give me that! (*Pages through it.*) All right. Here it is. (*Again with big gestures and great drama.*) Wing of bat and eye of toad. Pack your bags and hit the road! (*Looks expectantly at PRINCESSES who look expectantly back at her but, again, nothing happens. BEAUTY looks relieved.*)

FROG. (*Unsnapping frog head and removing it, smoothing back hair.*) Ah, that's more like it. I knew I had ears. (*Feels ears for reassurance.*) Yes, there they are. And I'm not hungry for flies anymore. (*All of the PRINCESSES, DWARFS and SOLDIERS go down on their haunches, start hopping around and saying "Ribet!" They don't do it so loud as to drown out the WITCHES. GRUB has hopped up on a box too.*)

SLUG. But they're supposed to disappear! Why aren't they disappearing?

FERMELDA. It was bad enough when they were princesses. Now they look like princesses and act like frogs! And the frog looks like a frog and talks like a prince!

GRUB. This is a fine kettle of fish!

FERMELDA, GRUB, SLUG. (*In tone of finally remembering.*) Fish! We forgot the fish! (*FERMELDA has whipped off hat, pulled out stuffed fish, throws it in pot. They jump down, grab sticks and start stirring.*)

FERMELDA. (*Hopefully.*) It's getting green ...

GRUB. (*Hopefully.*) I see lumps ...

SLUG. Oooh, lovely thick oil! Globs and globs of lovely, thick oil!

FERMELDA, GRUB, SLUG. It's perfect! (*All three are oblivious to the scene around them.*)

FROG. (*Taps closest WITCH on shoulder.*) Uh, excuse me. Excuse me? Do you think you could finish me up? I'm only half done. And aren't you going to do something about all this? (*Indicates all the hopping going on.*)

FERMELDA. (*Can hardly be bothered. Says it quickly to get rid of him.*) Oh ... Spider bites and werewolf laughter. Go somewhere and live happily ever after. (*EVERYONE is immediately recovered. Stand up, straighten themselves out, adjust crowns.*)

CINDERELLA. (*Going to Center Stage.*) Well, it is about time. (*Looks at watch.*) Oh! I can still make it! It's glass slipper time! (*Lifts skirts and charges off, Stage Left, scattering*

DWARFS.)

BEAUTY. (*Folding arms.*) Well, I'm not going. I don't care about your spells or your magic or your silly book. I'm here to stay.

FERMELDA. The Beast turns into a prince.

BEAUTY. He does?! When? How?

FERMELDA. When you fall in love with him.

BEAUTY. Oh. Well, that's asking a lot. (*Considers a moment.*) Maybe his table manners weren't all that disgusting. Which way? (*FERMELDA points Stage Left. BEAUTY hurries off, powdering nose and scattering DWARFS.*)

SNOW WHITE. (*Organizing DWARFS back into line, with some irritation.*) Come along now — we can be home just in time for supper. (*Heads off across Stage.*) Tonight I'm making your favorite — possum pot pie. (*Exits Right. DWARFS follow her in a line, delivering their lines at about Center Stage, then exiting right.*)

ALLERGIC. (*With dread.*) Oh no. I'm allergic to possum. (*Sneezing as he exits Right.*)

SARCASTIC. Yeah, it's really my favorite. I just love the slop. (*Exit Right.*)

STUPID. Me too. I just love the slop too. I think. Maybe. I'm not sure. I dunno ... (*Exit Right.*)

DEPRESSED. Just when things were looking up. I give up. What's the use? This is a pointless existence. (*Exit Right.*)

BORED. Anyway, we had it last week. I'm sick of it. Why can't we ever have anything different? (*Exit Right.*)

JUST PLAIN MEAN. Why did she have to find our cottage? (*Exit Right.*)

EXHAUSTED. I sure wish her prince would come. (*Exit Right.*)

PRINCESS/PEA. All right men! Positions! (*SOLDIERS*

hurry forward.) LIFT! (*They lift mattress.*) FORWARD MARCH! (*They march Offstage Left. The PRINCESS/PEA distracted by SLEEPING BEAUTY.*)

SLEEPING BEAUTY. Oh please don't take it! You have twenty-seven of them!

PRINCESS/PEA. Outta my way! Get your own mattress! And get yourself a can of peas! What kind of princess are you anyway? (*She marches Offstage Right. In a moment she comes charging back across stage screaming.*) HALT! HALT! HALT! (*Exits Stage Left.*)

SLEEPING BEAUTY. (*Looking sadly after them.*) Oh well. (*To FROG who has come Center Stage.*) So, you're a prince, huh?

FROG. (*Very pleased.*) Yes I am. And feeling better every minute. (*Removing frog hands.*) Well, see there. I knew I had hands.

SLEEPING BEAUTY. I'm Sleeping Beauty. (*They shake hands.*)

FROG. Charmed, I'm sure.

SLEEPING BEAUTY. (*Keeps on shaking hand, with more enthusiasm.*) Charmed? As in Charming? Prince Charming?

FROG. No. I'm not sure, but I think my name is Kermit.

SLEEPING BEAUTY. (*Drops his hand.*) Oh. Well, it's Prince Charming I'm waiting for. (*Sighs.*) And waiting. (*Sighs again.*) And waiting.

FROG. Charming? Oh, he's back at the castle.

SLEEPING BEAUTY. You know him?!

FROG. Sure. He's my cousin, once or twice removed. Tall guy. Broad shoulders. Rides around on a white horse.

SLEEPING BEAUTY. That's him!

FROG. Well, come on. I'll introduce you.

SLEEPING BEAUTY. Wow! I'm going to meet the prince.

This is too good to be true.

FROG. Of course this is too good to be true. This is a fairy tale. (*He offers his hand, she places her hand on his and they exit, Stage Right, in a royal manner.*)

FERMELDA. (*Looks around.*) Alone! We're alone!

SLUG. They're finally gone!

GRUB. Gone, gone, all gone! (*They all cackle.*)

FERMELDA. And now — at last — LUNCH! (*They each grab an old bowl or cup and eagerly scoop it into pot and take long, slurping sips.*)

FERMELDA. Ah ... not bad.

GRUB. Ah ... not bad at all.

SLUG. Could have used that dwarf though. (*They ALL nod in agreement but keep on sipping and slurping in true witch fashion. STORYTELLER enters, goes to Center Stage. WITCHES go on with their eating, pay no attention to her.*)

STORYTELLER.

Well, here we are.

At the end.

And nobody lost.

We all got to win.

The witches found their book.

So I'm off the hook.

Cinderella is dancing,

Beauty is romancing.

The frog who wasn't a frog isn't a frog anymore.

And they've all stopped hopping around on the floor.

Snow White is home cooking for those seven little men.

And the Princess and her Peas are marching again.

And Sleeping Beauty? I bet she

Will marry the prince and live happily.

So maybe the witches were right after all
About how many times we all should recall
The magic and mystery of this fairy tale stuff.
Once upon a time would never be enough.

CURTAIN

(Note: For final bow the cast can form two lines/one standing and one kneeling in front. When the curtain opens the PRINCESS/PEA shouts "BOW!" They all start bowing over and over again as the SOLDIERS did during the play. As the CURTAIN closes the PRINCESS/PEA shouts "STOP THAT BOWING!")

COSTUMES

STORYTELLER: A hodgepodge of pieces leftover from other character's costumes — ballgown, witch cape, frog hands, dwarf's beard, tiara, etc.

FERMELDA, SLUG, GRUB: Raggy black dresses, striped stockings, peaked hats. Fermelda's hat must be large enough to accommodate a large stuffed fish.

CINDERELLA, SNOW WHITE, BEAUTY: Long fancy ballgowns, gloves, lots of jewelry. Cinderella and Snow White wear tiaras.

PRINCESS AND THE PEA: Dressed like the other princesses but in a tea-length gown so her army boots and long johns show. She also wears a military uniform jacket.

SLEEPING BEAUTY: Has on a long gown that is a rumpled mess. Under it she wears a full-length pajama with feet. She carries a teddy bear and her tiara is always crooked.

DWARFS: Oversize shirts over a pillow all held in place by a big belt. Tights, short boots and long stocking caps. Each wears a long white beard.

SOLDIERS: Tunics worn over tights and turtlenecks. Caps. A pea emblem may be put on tunics and caps.

FROG: A frog suit with head and hands that can be easily removed Onstage.

PROPS

STORYTELLER: Large storybook.
FERMELDA: A large, stuffed fish inside her witch hat.
GRUB: A rock.
BEAUTY: A purse with a compact in it.
PRINCESS AND THE PEA: Large can of peas and a can opener.
SOLDIERS: Mattress.

THE LOST HALF-HOUR

Flexible cast of 25
Played on bare stage
30 minute playing time

The Lost Half-Hour was first performed by the Greenleaf 4-H Club in Green Bay, WI on November 2, 1991 with the following cast:

MOTHER TIME . . . . Heather Clancy
MOTHER . . . . Mickie Gibson
MATTHEW . . . . Mark Schultz
FERNANDO . . . . Rob Clancy
BOBO . . . . Jacob Geurts
PRINCESS PATTY . . . . Natalie Koltz
PRINCESS COURT 1 . . . . Lynn Kabat
PRINCESS COURT 2 . . . . Sarah Schultz
PRINCESS COURT 3 . . . . Holly Hibbard
TILDA . . . . Kristen Neuman
HORSE . . . . Jenny Gilson
STRANGER 1 . . . . Mike Kabat
STRANGER 2 . . . . Max Neuman
KING . . . . Chris Hibbard
KING COURT 1 . . . . Claire Wymelenberg
KING COURT 2 . . . . Rachel Dietz
KING COURT 3 . . . . Renee Schott
KING COURT 4 . . . . Abby Konopka
THREE O'CLOCK . . . . Ann Kabat
FOUR O'CLOCK . . . . Bobbi Jo Wiese
ELEVEN O'CLOCK . . . . Katie Mommaerts
NINE O'CLOCK . . . . Rebecca Shibler
OLD WOMAN . . . . Ellen Bowker
DRAGON . . . . Max Neuman

CHARACTERS

MOTHER TIME
MOTHER
MATTHEW
FERNANDO
BOBO
PRINCESS PATTY
PRINCESS COURT 1
PRINCESS COURT 2
PRINCESS COURT 3
PRINCESS COURT 4
TILDA
HORSE
STRANGER 1
STRANGER 2
KING
KING COURT 1
KING COURT 2
KING COURT 3
KING COURT 4
THREE O'CLOCK
FOUR O'CLOCK
ELEVEN O'CLOCK
NINE O'CLOCK
OLD WOMAN
DRAGON

Note: The number of Princess Courts and King Courts is flexible. Just redistribute the lines to accommodate more or fewer performers.

THE LOST HALF-HOUR

(Played on a bare stage.)

(Note: There is a lot of action in this play and it will be easier for the cast to learn — and fun for the audience to watch — if you are very precise and repetitive in your direction. For example, PRINCESS PATTY and her COURT always go On and Offstage in the same order, always start with right foot first, always have hands folded at waist, right hand over left hand, and always have their noses in the air. The KING's COURT, always uses march steps, always start with their right foot, always have arms straight down at their sides and always stay in a straight line behind the King. The cast gets very secure in their performances and the result is fun to watch.)

(At Rise: The satchel and the stick are lying Onstage in the appropriate spots. Stools for PRINCESS COURT 1, 2, 3, 4 are Up Left. The lost temper is Onstage but well out of the action. Ideally, it is on the bottom step of stairs leading up to the stage. MOTHER TIME stands Center Stage.)

MOTHER TIME. Once upon a time *(Strolls Stage Left.)* there was always time for a story ... *(Meets MOTHER entering Stage Left. MOTHER TIME exits Stage Left.)*

MOTHER. *(Enters Stage Left, carrying stool. To audience.)* About an old widow woman who had three sons. Oh *(Stops Center Stage, sets down stool, sits.)* the first two were clever enough.

MATTHEW. (*Enters Stage Right, carrying bucket.*) The cow is milked, Mother. (*Stands next to MOTHER, sets down bucket.*)

FERNANDO. (*Enters Stage Right, carrying hoe.*) The turnips are hoed, Mother. (*Stands next to MATTHEW, leans on hoe.*)

MOTHER. (*To audience. Exasperated.*) But the third son! (*MOTHER, MATTHEW and FERNANDO shake their heads and roll their eyes.*)

BOBO. (*Enters from Stage Left.*) The crack is corned, Mother. (*Stands next to MOTHER.*)

MOTHER. What, Bobo?

BOBO. The crack is corned. I didn't know if you meant the crack in the cow barn or the crack in the chicken coop or the crack in the pig shed, so I filled all three with corn. It was a big job — it took all the corn we had — but it's done. The animals seem very happy about it.

MOTHER. (*Jumps up.*) No! I said, crack the corn, crack the corn! Not corn the crack! Bobo, you simpleton! Though I give you a beating and a scolding a day, you stay foolish as ever! What am I to do with you? (*Sits, puts face in hands, MATTHEW pats her back.*)

FERNANDO. (*To audience.*) Now, it so happened that Princess Patty and her court (*PRINCESS PATTY and PRINCESS COURT 1, 2, 3, 4 enter Stage Right in a procession and cross stage behind other players. PRINCESS PATTY stops between MOTHER and BOBO. COURT stays in line behind her.*) were passing by that very morning and heard all the ruckus.

PRINCESS PATTY. I heard all the ruckus. Is the boy a criminal?

MOTHER. (*Jumps up.*) Worse! A simpleton! He doesn't crack the corn — he corns the crack!

PRINCESS PATTY. Ha ha! (*The laugh is done by saying the first "ha" in a high voice, the second "ha" in a lower voice and putting the head back and then forward with each "ha." The COURT mimics her precisely.)*

COURT 1, 2, 3, 4. Ha ha!

PRINCESS PATTY. I am amused. He will come with me.

MOTHER. With you?

PRINCESS PATTY. Life at court can be tedious. I need amusement. *(To BOBO.)* Come along ... *(To MOTHER.)* What is his name?

MOTHER. Bobo.

PRINCESS PATTY. *(Sarcastic.)* Bobo. It suits him. Come along, Bobo.

MOTHER. *(Takes BOBO's arm and pulls him closer to her.)* But he is, after all, my son. I can't just let him go.

PRINCESS PATTY. *(Looks bored, holds out hand to show a golden florin in it. Offers golden florin to MOTHER.)* A golden florin?

MOTHER. *(Grabs coin and shoves BOBO away.)* Sold!

MATTHEW. *(To audience.)* So, though Bobo didn't want to leave his home, he went to court with Princess Patty. *(MOTHER and FERNANDO have gone Offstage Right, admiring the coin. MATTHEW runs to catch up with them. PRINCESS PATTY, followed by PRINCESS COURT 2, 3 and 4, circle to Stage Left and back again to end up Center Stage. PRINCESS COURT 4 pulls BOBO along. He is waving to his family but they don't wave back. Each PRINCESS COURT picks up a stool from Upstage Left as they circle. When they get to Center Stage, PRINCESS PATTY sits on stool left behind by MOTHER. COURT arrange stools in line: 1 and 2 on PRINCESS' right and 3 and 4 on PRINCESS' left. BOBO standing next to 4. The PRINCESS sits. The others remain standing.)*

PRINCESS COURT 1. *(While others are circling the stage and arranging stools. To audience.)* Back at the castle it didn't take long for the courtiers, the footmen, the lackeys and even the lowliest of turnspits to discover how great a simpleton had arrived. (*PRINCESS COURT 1 hurries after others, following same route, picking up stool and putting it in line as indicated above.*)

PRINCESS COURT 4. Bobo, I have a need for a feather — from a white crow. (*PRINCESS and COURT giggle.*) Fetch me one! (*Sits.*)

BOBO. (*Eager to please, hurries Stage Right.*) Right away, mistress.

PRINCESS COURT 1. (*Grabs BOBO by the arm and spins him around.*) Bobo, go out to the meadow and pick me a spray of — yellow bluebells. (*PRINCESS and COURT giggle.*) Quickly! (*Sits.*)

BOBO. (*Hurries Stage Right.*) Oh yes, immediately, my lady.

PRINCESS COURT 3. (*Grabs BOBO by the arm and spins him around.*) Bobo, the cart is broken. To fix it we must have — a square wheel. (*PRINCESS and COURT giggle.*) Hurry now! (*Sits.*)

BOBO. (*Hurries Stage Right.*) I'm hurrying.

PRINCESS COURT 2. (*Grabs BOBO by arm and spins him around.*) Bobo, bring me a glass of — dry water. (*PRINCESS and COURT giggle.*) Immediately! (*Sits.*)

BOBO. (*Hurrying Stage Right.*) I'll be as quick as I can!

PRINCESS AND PRINCESS COURT 1, 2, 3, 4. (*Laugh in unison and turn on their stools so their backs are to the audience.*) Ha ha ha ha ha ha ha ha ha! (*The laughs should start with a high voice and end with a lower voice. Very precise.*)

TILDA. (*Mops Onstage Left. Mops across stage toward BOBO. To audience.*) The only one who was kind to Bobo was Tilda the kitchen maid who had been left at the castle when she was a baby. No one there was kind to her either.

BOBO. Tilda, I must have a glass of dry water.

TILDA. (*Stops mopping.*) Oh, Bobo, there is no such thing as dry water. They're making fun of you again.

BOBO. They are?

TILDA. When will you learn? They send you off on one wild goose chase after another — a white crow's feather, yellow bluebells, a square wheel. And today it's dry water.

BOBO. And I know where there's a dry well. I think I can get it there. (*Starting to leave.*)

TILDA. (*Stops him.*) Bobo, stay here by the fire, (*Positions him by an imaginary fire.*) have a cookie (*Gives him a cookie.*) and try not to be such a simpleton. (*Mops Offstage Right.*)

BOBO. I'll try. (*Eats cookie.*)

PRINCESS COURT 1. (*Turns on stool to face audience.*) The next morning, (*PRINCESS COURT 2, 3 and 4 turn on stools to face audience, all yawning and stretching.*) Princess Patty did not get up at her normal time. Instead of nine o'clock, she woke up at ...

PRINCESS PATTY. (*Turns on stool to face audience, yawning and stretching. Stands. Looks at watch.*) Nine thirty! Why, I've lost a half-hour this morning.

BOBO. (*Hurries over.*) Please, Your Highness, perhaps I can find it.

PRINCESS PATTY. Ha ha! Shall I let Bobo look for my lost half-hour?

PRINCESS COURT 1, 2, 3, 4. (*Stand.*) Ha ha!

PRINCESS COURT 1. Yes, yes! Let Bobo find the lost half-hour. (*PRINCESS and COURT giggle.*)

PRINCESS COURT 2. I'll give him my horse. She's old and she's slow but she's good enough for Bobo. (*Drags HORSE on from Stage Right. PRINCESS and COURT giggle. HORSE stands next to BOBO.*)

PRINCESS COURT 3. (*Picks up satchel from floor behind stool.*) I'll give him this ragged old satchel. I hope the half-hour fits in it. (*Puts satchel over BOBO's shoulder. PRINCESS and COURT giggle.*)

PRINCESS COURT 4. (*Picks up stick from floor behind stool.*) And I'll give him this stick — for a weapon. (*Puts stick in satchel. PRINCESS and COURT giggle.*)

PRINCESS COURT 1. (*To audience. TILDA mops Onstage Right.*) So, in less time than it takes to tell about it, Bobo was ready for his journey.

BOBO. (*Sees TILDA Stage Right and hurries over to her. HORSE follows him.*) Tilda! I'm off on a great quest to find Her Highness' lost half-hour.

TILDA. (*Stops mopping.*) Not again.

BOBO. The princess herself has commanded it.

PRINCESS COURT 2. (*To audience.*) Tilda shook her head (*TILDA shakes her head.*) and said ...

TILDA. Oh Bobo.

PRINCESS COURT 3. (*To audience.*) But seeing that she could not dissuade him, patted him on the back (*TILDA pats BOBO on the back.*) gave him a bag of cookies (*TILDA gives BOBO a bag of cookies from her apron pocket. He puts it in his satchel.*) and said ...

TILDA. I wish you the best of fortune, Bobo.

BOBO. Thank you, Tilda. When I come back I will bring you a splendid present.

TILDA. (*Mopping Offstage Right.*) So Bobo went with his horse to the castle gate. (*BOBO and HORSE cross to Stage Left in front of PRINCESS and COURT.*)

PRINCESS AND PRINCESS COURT 1, 2, 3, 4. (*Sarcastic.*) Goodbye Bobo!

PRINCESS PATTY.   Do not fail to bring back the lost half-hour!

BOBO.   I'll try! Goodbye! (*BOBO and HORSE circle Stage Left and end up back at Center Stage.*)

PRINCESS AND PRINCESS COURT 1, 2, 3, 4.   (*Pick up stools and go Stage Right, PRINCESS first and COURT following her in order. They laugh as they go.*) Ha ha ha ha ha ha ha ha ha ha! (*PRINCESS exits. COURT stands in line Stage Right.*)

PRINCESS COURT 1.   (*To audience.*) So, Bobo and his horse set off and traveled ...

PRINCESS COURT 2.   (*To audience.*) Over mountains ... (*BOBO and HORSE Center Stage. Take big step forward in unison as though stepping over a mountain.*)

PRINCESS COURT 3.   (*To audience.*) Through jungles ... (*BOBO and HORSE crouch, take one step forward in unison while spreading arms in front of them as though pushing through a jungle.*)

PRINCESS COURT 4. (*To audience.*) And around ... (*BOBO and HORSE walk in unison in a small circle, about eight little steps, ending up in same spot they started.*) an ocean and there they came to a road where ... (*PRINCESS COURT 1, 2, 3, 4 exit Stage Right.*)

STRANGER 1.   (*Enters Stage Right. Very frantic, running fingers through hair, almost having a breakdown. To audience.*) As often happens with travelers, they met a stranger. (*Crosses stage, meeting BOBO and HORSE Center Stage.*)

BOBO.   Excuse me, sir, I am looking for a lost half-hour. Have you seen one?

STRANGER 1.   A lost half-hour? Don't waste my time. I've lost something much more important. I've lost my reputation. You haven't seen a lost reputation lying about, have you? It was very dignified and wore tortoise shell glasses. (*BOBO and*

HORSE look at each other and shake heads.)

BOBO. No.

STRANGER 1. (*Going Offstage Left. To audience.*) The first stranger had no more passed out of sight ... (*Exits. Stage Left.*)

STRANGER 2. (*Enters Stage Left. In a very bad temper. To audience.*) When another stranger appeared. (*Crosses stage, meeting BOBO and HORSE Center Stage.*)

BOBO. If you please, sir, I am looking for a lost half-hour. Have you seen one?

STRANGER 2. (*Rage.*) A half-hour! No, I haven't seen your half-hour! I wouldn't tell you if I had. What's more, I don't want to see it. I'm looking for something I've lost myself. I've lost my temper! I lost it two years ago in this spot and haven't been able to find it anywhere since. (*Grabs BOBO by throat.*) Answer me! Have you seen a lost temper anywhere? It's about the size of a large melon and has sharp little points. (*BOBO and HORSE shake heads, frightened.*)

BOBO. No!

STRANGER 2. (*Pushes them aside. To audience.*) And, of course, when there are two strangers, there is always... (*Exits Stage Right.*)

KING. (*Enters Stage Right. Sad. To audience.*) A king.

KING COURT 1, 2, 3, 4. (*Enter in a straight line behind him. To audience.*) And his court. (*KING and COURT cross stage, meeting BOBO and HORSE at Center Stage.*)

BOBO. Pardon me, I am looking for a lost half-hour. Have you seen one?

KING. A lost half-hour? No. I am king of all these lands and I am quite sure it has not been seen in my dominions. Would you mind asking, as you go through the world, for news of my little daughter?

BOBO. (*To audience.*) Here, the poor old king took out a great green handkerchief and wiped his eyes. (*The KING does just that.*)

KING. She was stolen one midsummer morn fifteen years ago. Find her, worthy sir, and an immense reward will be yours. (*Crosses to Stage Left. COURT follows. KING exits. COURT stands in line at Stage Left.*)

KING COURT 1. (*To audience. Slowly, to match weariness of BOBO and HORSE.*) So, though they were very weary, Bobo and his horse traveled over more mountains ... (*BOBO and HORSE do mountain action, but very tired this time.*)

KING COURT 2. (*To audience. Tired.*) Through more jungles ... (*BOBO and HORSE do jungle action. Tired.*)

KING COURT 3. (*To audience. Tired.*) And around one last ... (*BOBO and HORSE do ocean action. Tired.*) ocean but not a sign of the lost half-hour did he find though he asked thousands of people ...

BOBO. (*Puts hands to mouth and shouts.*) Has anybody seen a lost half-hour?

ALL. (*Cast On and Offstage.*) No!

KING COURT 4. Along the way. And then one day they came to ... (*KING COURT 1, 2, 3, 4 exit Stage Left.*)

BOBO. (*BOBO and HORSE almost step off edge of stage.*) Whoa! (*Pulls HORSE back.*) The horizon! (*Looking over edge.*) That's quite a drop. (*Back away from edge a little. MOTHER TIME enters Stage Left, peering across stage to Stage Right, shading eyes, doesn't see BOBO.*) Well, Horse, I don't know what else to do. We have traveled to the end of the world and asked everyone we've seen about the lost half-hour. (*MOTHER TIME bumps into BOBO.*) Everyone but you!

MOTHER TIME. (*Startled.*) What are you doing here? Shoo! Go away! (*To Offstage Left.*) Come along, girls! (*From

Stage Left, FOUR O'CLOCK enters carrying "Lost And Found" box, sets it down so audience can't read it, starts doing warm-up exercises. ELEVEN O'CLOCK carries on low stool. NINE O'CLOCK carries on small pan. They set items on floor and sit next to them.)

BOBO. But I just want to ask you a question, if you have a minute to spare.

MOTHER TIME. A minute to spare! Just because I'm Mother Time doesn't mean I have a minute to spare. I need all my minutes.

BOBO. You're Mother Time?

MOTHER TIME. Yes. How do you do. Go away.

BOBO. Could I ask you a question? I'm sure you'll know the answer.

MOTHER TIME. I promise you I won't. And even if I did -- you're in the way! *Step aside!* (*Pushes BOBO and HORSE aside.*) The hours are changing!

BOBO. They are?

MOTHER TIME. Of course they are. My twelve sons are the hours of the night. My twelve daughters are the hours of the day. Every hour, one after another, they walk around the world, staying away from the edge, of course. (*THREE O'CLOCK enters Stage Right, walking along edge of stage very tired.*)

BOBO. That's what controls time?

MOTHER TIME. We're not sure but we think so. Oh, here comes Three O'Clock now.

THREE O'CLOCK. Hi Mom.

MOTHER TIME. (*Sympathetically.*) Hello dear. Go soak your feet.

THREE O'CLOCK. I will. (*Goes to stool, sits, removes shoes, soaks feet.*)

FOUR O'CLOCK. (*Walking back the same way THREE*

O'CLOCK came from.) Bye Mom.

MOTHER TIME. (*Very concerned.*) Bye dear. How are your blisters today?

FOUR O'CLOCK. About the same as yesterday. (*Continues across stage and exits Stage Right.*)

MOTHER TIME. Poor babies. All that walking, you know.

HORSE. They should have a horse, such as myself. Then they could ride.

BOBO. (*Surprised.*) Ride?

MOTHER TIME. No, no. That would cause time to go by too fast.

HORSE. Not with me. I'm old and slow but if I'm good enough for Bobo I'd be good enough for you.

BOBO. I was supposed to ride you?

MOTHER TIME. Well, normally I don't deal in livestock, but my poor babies' feet. (*Reluctantly takes out change purse. Suspicious.*) How much?

BOBO. (*To HORSE.*) Would you like to stay?

HORSE. Very much. Life at court can be tedious and travel agrees with me.

BOBO. Then stay you shall. (*To MOTHER TIME.*) No charge. She was a gift to me and she is now a gift to you. (*Presents HORSE to MOTHER TIME.*)

MOTHER TIME. (*Very glad to put away change purse.*) Very generous, I'm sure.

BOBO. (*Pretending to leave but stalling.*) Well, I guess I'll be on my way, see if there's anybody out there who maybe would have a spare minute so I can ask my question ...

MOTHER TIME. Well, since you were so nice about the horse ... (*Reluctantly.*) What's your question?

BOBO. (*Hurries back.*) I'm looking for a lost half-hour. Have you seen it?

MOTHER TIME. Well, we do have a lost and found. Girls? (*ELEVEN O'CLOCK and NINE O'CLOCK bring over "Lost And Found" box so audience can now read it. Holding it for her.*) Let's see … (*Rummaging through it.*) Time wasted, time squandered, daylight savings time … ah! Here's a half-hour.

ONE O'CLOCK. (*To audience.*) And she lifted out a beautiful black ebony box. (*MOTHER TIME lifts out small box. BOBO reaches for it.*)

MOTHER TIME. (*Holding it away from BOBO.*) Ah, ah, ah! You'll have to identify it! (*ELEVEN O'CLOCK and NINE O'CLOCK step aside with "Lost and Found" box.*)

BOBO. (*Carefully.*) It is nine o'clock to nine thirty on the morning of twelfth of August of this year.

MOTHER TIME. (*Looks at bottom of box.*) You're in luck — this is it! (*Very cautionary.*) Now! The half-hour lies inside. Don't peek at it or open the box until you're ready to use it. If you do, the half-hour will fly away and disappear. They can be very independent. I can't be held responsible.

BOBO. I'll be careful. (*MOTHER TIME hands him the box. He places it carefully over his heart and holds it there. He tries to see what else might be in the "Lost And Found" box.*) You wouldn't have a lost reputation in there? Or a lost temper? Or a lost baby girl?

MOTHER TIME. (*Blocking his view.*) No, no, no! Just time! Now go away! Fly! Goodbye! (*Takes "Lost and Found" box and HORSE, goes Stage Left and looks disapproving.*)

THREE O'CLOCK. (*Eagerly comes forward. Stands next to BOBO.*) But I know of a lost reputation.

NINE AND ONE O'CLOCK. No!

THREE O'CLOCK. Yes! (*To BOBO.*) I was passing by — it was exactly eight after three when it happened. It broke into a thousand pieces and the pieces were picked up by the man's neighbors and taken home.

ELEVEN O'CLOCK. (*Eagerly pushes THREE O'CLOCK aside and takes her place.*) And it was just eleven thirty-nine when I saw a gentleman lose his temper!

THREE AND NINE O'CLOCK. No!

ELEVEN O'CLOCK. Yes! And a very nasty temper it was. It rolled into the deep grasses along the roadside and is still there for all I know. I'd stay away from it if I were you. You never know when those things are going to go off.

NINE O'CLOCK. (*Eagerly pushes ELEVEN O'CLOCK aside and takes her place.*) And I saw a baby girl taken from the King With The Green Handkerchief's castle.

THREE AND ELEVEN O'CLOCK. No!

NINE O'CLOCK. Yes! (*To BOBO.*) The bad fairies did it. Nine after nine it was — and by nine fifty-nine she was on the doorstep of Princess Patty. I still see her when I pass that way. Her name is Tilda. She is a kitchen maid.

BOBO. You've answered all my questions. How can I thank you?

THREE O'CLOCK. (*With urgency.*) Hurry home!

ELEVEN O'CLOCK. Don't waste any time!

NINE O'CLOCK. Make every second count!

MOTHER TIME. And don't come back! (*Exits with "Lost and Found" box and HORSE. THREE, NINE and ELEVEN O'CLOCK form line at Stage Left. Speak quickly.*)

THREE O'CLOCK. (*To audience. Urgent.*) So, Bobo hurried home to the other side of the world, being careful to stay away from the edge, going over mountains ... (*BOBO does mountain action quickly.*)

ELEVEN O'CLOCK. (*To audience. Urgent.*) Through jungles ... (*BOBO does jungle action quickly.*)

NINE O'CLOCK. (*To audience. Urgent.*) And around ...

(*BOBO does ocean action quickly.*) an ocean and finally back to the very same road he had traveled so long ago. (*THREE, ELEVEN and NINE O'CLOCK pick up stool, pan, shoes and socks and exit Stage Left.*)

STRANGER 1. (*Enters Stage Left. Still frantic. To audience.*) And there was the first stranger. (*Continues to Center Stage.*)

BOBO. Sir! Your reputation has been broken into one thousand pieces. Collect the pieces from your neighbors and it will be whole again.

STRANGER 1. But what if they won't give them back?

BOBO. Hmmmm. Trade them — for cookies. (*Hands him bag of cookies from satchel.*)

STRANGER 1. (*Calms down.*) That is good advise. You are very wise — and generous. Thank you. (*Continues Stage Right. To audience.*) And he hurried off to his neighbors' houses with the bag of cookies. (*Exits Stage Right.*)

STRANGER 2. (*Enters Stage Right, very angry. To audience.*) And there was the second stranger! (*Continues to Center Stage.*)

BOBO. Sir!

STRANGER 2. What?!

BOBO. Your temper is in the grass — (*Looks, points.*) There!

STRANGER 2. My temper! (*Picks it up, demeanor immediately pleasant.*) At last.

BOBO. A temper is a vile thing. It can explode at any moment. But, you know, if you give it away, you'll never lose it again.

STRANGER 2. True. You are very wise. Will you dispose of it for me?

BOBO. Certainly. (*Puts lost temper in his satchel.*)

STRANGER 2.   (*Hands in pockets, whistling, happy. Continues Stage Left. To KING.*) Morning. (*Exits Stage Left.*)

KING. (*Enters Stage Left. To audience.*) And, finally, there was the king.

KING COURT 1, 2, 3, 4. (*Enter in line behind KING. To audience.*) And his court. (*KING and COURT continue to Center Stage.*)

BOBO. King! I have the best of all possible news. Your daughter is found. She is the kitchen maid Tilda in the castle of Princess Patty.

KING. Oh, my joy knows no bounds! What is your name?

BOBO. Bobo.

KING. (*Impressed.*) Bobo. It suits you. I hereby declare you Lord Bobo of the Sapphire Hills ... (*KING COURT 1 presents medal. Stands to BOBO's right.*) Marquis of the Mountains of the Moon ... (*KING COURT 2 presents medal. Stands to KING COURT 1's right.*) Prince of the Valley of Golden Apples... (*KING COURT 3 presents medal. Stands to KING COURT 2's right.*) and Lord Seneschal of the proud city of Zizz. (*KING COURT 4 presents medal. Stands to KING COURT 3's right.*)

BOBO. Thank you.

KING. (*Starting to leave.*) And now I'm off to collect my daughter.

BOBO. (*Stops him.*) Wait — I'll show you the way. You have to go over the mountains ... (*Does mountain action.*)

KING AND COURT 1, 2, 3, 4. Over the mountains ... (*Do mountain action in unison.*)

BOBO. Through the jungles ... (*Does jungle action.*)

KING AND COURT 1, 2, 3, 4. Through the jungles ... (*Do jungle action in unison.*)

BOBO. And around ... (*Does ocean action.*)

KING AND COURT 1, 2, 3, 4. And around ... (*Do ocean action in unison.*) ... an ocean.

BOBO. (*Leading them Stage Left.*) And here we are at the borders of the land of Princess Patty.

KING COURT 1. (*As they follow BOBO. To audience.*) And there, strange to say, black mourning banners ...

KING COURT 2. ... hung from the trees ...

KING COURT 3. ... and on every door

KING COURT 4. In every village. And they stopped at a cottage where ...

OLD WOMAN. (*Enters Stage Left with low stool, sits.*) An old woman sat weeping. (*Puts face in hands, weeps.*)

KING. What is the matter, my good woman?

KING COURT 4. (*To audience.*) Asked the king.

OLD WOMAN. Oh, sire, evil days have befallen our happy kingdom. (*PRINCESS PATTY and PRINCESS COURT 1, 2, 3, 4 enter Stage Right and stand in line, staying on right side of stage. BOBO, KING, KING COURT 1, 2, 3, 4 listen intently to OLD WOMAN's story and are oblivious to action in "the garden of the palace."*) This morning a terrible dragon ...

ALL. (*Cast On and Offstage. DRAGON enters Stage Right on the word "Woooosssh!!"*) Woooooossssh!!!!

OLD WOMAN. Alighted in the garden of the palace and told the princess ...

DRAGON. I command you to provide me with a servant to cook my grub and mop my lair.

PRINCESS PATTY. (*To PRINCESS COURT 1.*) Tell this lizard I do not take commands. I give them.

DRAGON. Then your fields and villages and the castle itself will be burned black to the dirt by this lizard. Have someone here in the garden at two o'clock. Or else. (*Exits Stage Right. TILDA mops Onstage Right.*)

PRINCESS. In all the land there is no one foolish enough to become servant to that trash.

OLD WOMAN. (*To audience.*) Said the princess.

TILDA. I'll do it.

PRINCESS AND PRINCESS COURT 1, 2, 3, 4. Why?

TILDA. Life at court can be tedious and this way the whole land won't be destroyed. Just me.

PRINCESS COURT 1. There is someone foolish enough.

PRINCESS. And one is all we need. (*To TILDA.*) Be in the garden at two o'clock sharp. (*TILDA has stopped mopping.*) And don't stop mopping. It isn't two o'clock yet. (*PRINCESS and PRINCESS COURT 1, 2, 3, 4 cross stage, exit Stage Left TILDA mops Offstage Right.*)

OLD WOMAN. And so it is that poor little Tilda the kitchen maid will be carried off by the dragon at two o'clock and it is for her that we mourn, the brave, fearless little soul. (*Weeps.*)

BOBO. Tilda!

KING. My baby!

KING COURT 1. (*To audience.*) And though it was a great distance, they all ran (*BOBO, KING, KING COURT 2, 3, 4 and OLD WOMAN run in circle ending up at Stage Right.*) the rest of the way in a great charge, arriving breathless at the palace garden at ... (*KING COURT 1 runs in circle following same route and ending up with others who are all breathless and panting.*)

KING COURT 4. (*Looking at watch.*) Two twenty-nine!

KING. There's nobody here.

OLD WOMAN. (*Points up in sky over audience.*) There she goes! There's Tilda in the claws of the monstrous dragon, just a little smokey speck disappearing in the southern sky.

BOBO, KING AND KING COURT 1, 2, 3, 4. (*Looking where OLD WOMAN is pointing. Sadly.*) Aaaaahhh.

OLD WOMAN. (*To BOBO.*) If only you'd been here sooner, you could have saved her.

BOBO. Sooner? How much sooner?

OLD WOMAN. Oh, about a half-hour.

BOBO. (*To audience.*) So, Bobo took a deep breath ... (*He takes deep breath. The OTHERS form a group around him to see what is going to happen. NOTE: Each character who describes what happens as the box is opened and the half-hour flies out and so on should do so with a sense of wonder.*)

MOTHER. (*Enters Stage Right. To audience.*) And slowly opened the beautiful black ebony box. (*Joins group.*)

MATTHEW. (*Enters Stage Right. To audience.*) And something like a white winged flame ... (*Joins group.*)

ALL. (*ALL follow the "winged flame" as it shoots from the box to a point straight over their heads.*) Zing!

FERNANDO. (*Enters Stage Right. To audience.*) Flew hissing through the air to the sun! (*Joins group.*)

ALL. (*In unison, follow a pattern of movement with each "zing" as "winged flame" flies about the sky.*) Zing, zing, zing, zing, zing, zing, zing!

PRINCESS PATTY. (*Enters Stage Left. To audience.*) As for the sun itself, it turned round like a cartwheel! (*Joins group.*)

ALL. (*In unison, point with right arm to "the sun", a spot in the left side of the "sky".*) Ah!

PRINCESS COURT 1. (*Enter Stage Left. To audience.*) And hissing ... (*ALL begin hissing and continue to entrance of PRINCESS COURT 3.*) like ten thousand rockets ... (*Joins group.*)

PRINCESS COURT 2. (*Enters Stage Left. To audience.*) It rolled back along the sky to the east. (*ALL in unison make big circles with pointing arms following "sun" as it rolls from left to right. Freeze with arms pointing to the right side of the "sky".*)

PRINCESS COURT 3. (*Enters Stage Left. To audience.*) And the hands of all the clocks and watches and sundials and timepieces in all the kingdom whirred back from two thirty ... (*Joins group.*)

ALL. (*In unison, lower arms from pointing position to straight down at sides.*) Whiiiiirrrrrrrr.

PRINCESS COURT 4. (*Enters Stage Left. To audience.*) To two o'clock. And sure enough ... (*Joins group.*)

ALL. (*Split into two separate groups, stepping away from the center of stage to reveal TILDA mopping behind them. The cast should take three steps backwards — one for each word.*) There was Tilda.

TILDA. (*Straightens up.*) Almost two o'clock. I guess I can stop mopping.

BOBO. (*Hurries over to her.*) Tilda!

TILDA. Bobo!

BOBO. I've brought you a splendid present.

ALL. (*To audience. In low, ominous tones.*) Bonnnnng. Bonnnnng. (*DRAGON enters Stage Right.*) Wooooossssshh!! (*EVERYONE but BOBO, KING and TILDA cower in fear.*)

DRAGON. (*Looking at TILDA. With a snarl.*) Ah!

TILDA. (*Disappointed.*) Ah.

KING. (*Bravely draws sword, challenging DRAGON.*) Ah!

KING COURT 1. (*To audience.*) And the king ...

BOBO. Ah! (*Bravely draws stick from satchel, challenging DRAGON.*)

KING COURT 2. (*To audience.*) And Bobo

TILDA. (*Bravely draws mop, challenging DRAGON.*) Ah! (*KING, BOBO and TILDA are now in classic fencing position with swords pointing at DRAGON.*)

KING COURT 3. (*To audience.*) And Tilda fought bravely.

ALL. (*KING, BOBO and TILDA make fencing motions in

unison with each "fight".) Fight, fight, fight, fight, fight!

KING COURT 4. (*To audience.*) But their weapons would not pierce (*KING, BOBO and TILDA in unison 'stab' DRAGON.*) The tough hide of the dragon. (*All three weapons clatter to the ground.*)

DRAGON. (*Snide.*) Ha ha ha.

OLD WOMAN. (*To audience.*) And the dragon grabbed Tilda and pulled ... (*DRAGON grabs TILDA's right arm, pulls once and freezes. EVERYONE on right side of stage does the pulling motion and freezes.*) And the king grabbed Tilda and pulled ... (*KING grabs TILDA's left arm, pulls once and freezes. EVERYONE on left side of stage does the pulling motion and freezes.*) And Bobo searched frantically for a weapon ... (*BOBO at Center Stage looking frantically through satchel.*) and found ...

BOBO. (*Brings out lost temper.*) The lost temper!

DRAGON. (*Sees lost temper. Drops TILDA's arm.*) What's that? It looks like a large melon with sharp little points. My favorite! (*Grabs it.*)

BOBO. (*To audience.*) And the dragon bit into it and there was a perfectly terrific ...

ALL. (*DRAGON "bites". ALL clap hands over ears.*) BOOOOMMMMMM!!!! (*DRAGON's eyes get very big. Freezes.*)

BOBO. (*To audience.*) Like seven million balloons had blown up all at once but it wasn't seven million balloons.

DRAGON. (*To audience. Stunned. Holds up one finger.*) It was one dragon.

BOBO. (*To audience.*) Who'd been blown into seven million pieces and only one of the pieces ...

DRAGON. (*To audience. Removes nail. Hands it to BOBO.*) A tiny bit of claw.

BOBO. (*To audience.*) Was ever found. (*DRAGON sinks to ground.*)

ALL. Whew!

KING. Tilda, you are my daughter and you are a real princess.

TILDA. Really? What a splendid present.

KING. And you, Bobo, you are not only wise. You are brave. Kneel. (*BOBO kneels. With great ceremony.*) I confer upon you the Grand Cross of the Order of the Black Cat. (*Hangs very impressive medal around BOBO's neck.*)

ALL. (*Very impressed.*) Ocooooh!

BOBO. (*Stands.*) Thank you.

DRAGON. (*To audience. Getting up. Disgusted.*) You may be sure they all shouted ... (*Exits Stage Right.*)

ALL. Hooray!

MOTHER. (*To audience.*) And Princess Patty and her court apologized to Bobo for having treated him so shabbily.

PRINCESS PATTY AND COURT. (*Very sheepish.*) We're sorry.

BOBO. It's all right. Just don't let it happen again.

PRINCESS PATTY. (*To audience.*) And Bobo's mother and brothers apologized to Bobo for having treated him so shabbily.

MOTHER, MATTHEW AND FERNANDO. (*Very sheepish.*) We're sorry.

BOBO. It's all right. Just don't let it happen again. And ... (*Holding out hand.*) give me back the golden florin. (*MOTHER hesitates.*) Come on. (*She gives it to him.*)

MATTHEW. (*To audience.*) And Bobo returned the golden florin ...

FERNANDO. (*To audience.*) To the princess.

BOBO. (*Hands golden florin to PRINCESS PATTY.*) You spent a golden florin for a simpleton. You didn't get one.

OLD WOMAN. (*All the rest of the lines in the play are spoken to the audience.*) And they all ...

ALL. (*Quickly form two lines, staggered so no one is blocked from the audience. TILDA, KING and BOBO should be in center of front row.*) all of them traveled over the mountains ... (*Do mountain action.*) through the jungles ... (*Do jungle action.*) and around ... (*Do ocean action.*) an ocean.

KING. And back to the king's land where there was a wonderful feast and great rejoicing.

ALL. Yah!

PRINCESS PATTY. And when it was all over Tilda and Bobo were married.

ALL. (*TILDA and BOBO step forward, link arms. TILDA pulls bouquet from pocket. Each motion should be on one of the musical tones. To the tune of "Here Comes The Bride."*) Da dum da-dum!

FERNANDO. And there was another wonderful feast and more great rejoicing.

ALL. Yah, yah!

PRINCESS COURT 3. (*Sadly.*) And after some years when the old king died ...

ALL. (*KING takes off crown and hands it to OLD WOMAN, turns away, bows head and exits. Each motion should be on one of the musical tones. To the tune of a slow funeral dirge.*) Da dum da dum.

OLD WOMAN. They ruled his kingdom, the proud land of Zizz, and became known as ... (*Has slipped apart the paper crowns. Crowns TILDA.*) Queen Tilda ...

TILDA. (*Puts clenched fist over heart. Bravely.*) The Lionhearted.

OLD WOMAN. (*Crowns BOBO.*) And King Bobo ...

BOBO. (*Folds arms. Wisely.*) The Wise.

TILDA. And ... (*EVERYONE but TILDA and BOBO turn, fold hands behind their backs and walk off in unison. TILDA and*

BOBO speak their last lines slowly, as the last lines of a story are told, so the players can slowly stroll off.) so it was for so many years all together ...

BOBO. That we can't count them. (*TILDA and BOBO turn, put hands behind their backs and stroll off, exiting at opposite sides of the stage.*)

MOTHER TIME. (*Without any break in dialogue. Enters Stage Left.*) And in that happy land, when time passed, it passed slowly so there was always time for a story ... (*Meets MOTHER entering Stage Right. Exits Stage Right.*)

MOTHER. (*Enters carrying stool. Goes Center Stage.*) About an old widow woman who had three sons. (*Sits.*) Oh, the first two were clever enough. (*Slow curtain begins.*)

MATTHEW. (*Enters Stage Right with bucket.*) The cow is milked, Mother. (*Sets down bucket, stands next to MOTHER.*)

FERNANDO. (*Enters Stage Right with hoe.*) The turnips are hoed, Mother. (*Leans on hoe, stands next to MATTHEW.*)

MOTHER. (*To the audience. Exasperated.*) But the third son! (*MOTHER, MATTHEW and FERNANDO shake their heads and roll their eyes.*)

CURTAIN

COSTUMES

MOTHER TIME: Mother Goose-style dress, apron and bonnet.

MOTHER: Peasant-type long skirt, blouse, shawl, kerchief on hair, bare feet.

MATTHEW, FERNANDO, BOBO: Peasant-type worn-out pants, baggy shirts, bare feet. Bobo should be more ragged than the other two.

PRINCESS PATTY, PRINCESS COURTS: Long, pretty prom or bridesmaid dresses. Princess Patty wears a crown. Try to have Princess Courts look the same — perhaps all in blue dresses and with the same hairstyle.

TILDA: Peasant-type long skirt, blouse, apron with a big pocket, kerchief on hair, bare feet.

HORSE: Plain sweatshirt and sweatpants in either black, brown or gray. Man's felt hat with horse ears stapled to it.

STRANGER 1: Very disheveled business suit, shirt and tie.

STRANGER 2: Rough dirty work clothes.

KING, KING COURTS: Black pants, shirts and socks. Tunics. King's should have extra trim to set him apart. King wears two paper crowns, one worn inside the other so it looks like one.

THREE, FOUR, ELEVEN and NINE O'CLOCK: Black pants, shirts and socks. A big white cardboard clock reading the appropriate time hung around neck with black ribbon.

OLD WOMAN: Black long skirt, blouse and a shawl worn over head. Bare feet.

DRAGON: Black pants, shirt and socks. Add green cape with sequins or other trim to suggest a dragon.

PROPS

MOTHER TIME: Change purse in pocket.

MOTHER: Stool.

MATTHEW: Bucket.

FERNANDO: Hoe.

PRINCESS COURT 1: Golden florin — a cardboard circle wrapped in gold foil.

PRINCESS COURT 3: Roomy, ragged burlap sack with shoulder strap.

PRINCESS COURT 4: A thick stick about a yard long.

PRINCESS COURT 1, 2, 3, 4: Each needs a stool. Do not have to be same style but height should be about the same and all should be a little lower than the one shared by Mother and Princess Patty. All the stools used in the play should be the same color, probably white.

TILDA: Rag floor mop. Cookie, paper bag of cookies and a bouquet of plastic flowers — all in apron pocket.

STRANGER 2: The lost temper — an old volleyball with nails pounded halfway into it and spray-painted black and brown.

KING: Sword, a large bright green handkerchief, a very impressive medal hanging on a ribbon.

KING COURT 1, 2, 3, 4: Each needs a medal to present to Bobo, either by hanging it around his neck on a ribbon or attaching it to Velcro sewn to his shirt.

FOUR O'CLOCK: Large cardboard box labeled "lost and found". Inside there is a small, shiny black box.

ELEVEN O'CLOCK: A low stool.

NINE O'CLOCK: A small pan for soaking feet.

OLD WOMAN: A low stool. May use same one as Eleven O'Clock.

MURDER AT THE GREY'S HOUND MANSION
Maxine Holmgren

Mystery, High School/ Community Theatre / 5f, 3m / Simple Set
This is a mysterious comedy (or a comical mystery) that will have everyone howling with laughter.

The eccentric owner of Grey's Hound Mansion has been murdered. The cast gathers at the gloomy mansion for the reading of the will. Lightning lights up the stage as thunder and barking dogs greet the wacky characters that arrive. Each one is a suspect, and each one suspects another. Mixed metaphors and alliterations will have the audience barking up the wrong tree until the mystery is solved.

Baker's Plays
7611 Sunset Blvd.
Los Angeles, CA 90046
Phone: 323-876-0579
Fax: 323-876-5482

BAKERSPLAYS.COM